Sir James Arbory was everything that Pandora most disliked and disapproved of—haughty, rich, owning far more than his fair share of the world's goods. But he also had far more than his fair share of charm—something that had disastrous results for Pandora, who promptly fell in love with him. And she had gone out of her way to ensure that he would never look at her twice!

SUMMER FIRE

BY

SALLY WENTWORTH

MILLS & BOON LIMITED
15–16 BROOK'S MEWS
LONDON W1A 1DR

First published 1981
Australian copyright 1981
Philippine copyright 1981
This edition 1981

© Sally Wentworth 1981

ISBN 0 263 73609 1

Set in Monophoto Times 10 on 11½ pt.

Made and printed in Great Britain by
Richard Clay (The Chaucer Press) Ltd,
Bungay, Suffolk

CHAPTER ONE

THE roar of the high-powered engine reverberated harshly against the walls of the centuries-old cottages as the black-leather-clad motorcyclist accelerated down the long hill that led into the quiet Cotswold village of Arbory Magna. The rider slowed down to negotiate the twists in the narrow road between the stone walls of the houses, weathered to a warm honey colour and drowsing sleepily in the still sunshine of an afternoon in early summer. At the Arbory Arms, which served as the village's only pub, two elderly men sat outside at a wooden table, playing dominoes and each with a pint glass of dark brown ale conveniently near to hand. They looked up as the motorcycle came to a stop at the kerb, the noise of the engine dying down, but the big black and silver machine still throbbing with life between the rider's legs, ready to roar away again at the smallest pressure of hand and foot.

The motorcyclist raised a gauntleted hand to lift the dark-tinted vizor of the astronaut-like helmet and regarded the two men. 'Can you tell me the way to Abbot's Arbory?' the rider called in a voice muffled by the chin-guard of the helmet.

For a moment the two drinkers stared silently, taking in the motorcyclist's fronded leather jacket decorated with chrome studs in the shape of a skull and crossbones on the back, the tight trousers and the high boots, then one roused himself to point down the road. 'You go out of the village and up t'hill t'other side,' he answered in a heavy dialect. 'Go on for about half a mile and you'll come t'the gates of East Lodge. You can't miss it. There be big stone pillars.' .

'Thanks.' The rider raised a hand in acknowledgement and gunned the machine into roaring life again, surging off in the direction the men had given.

Even before it had disappeared round the first corner the two drinkers had exchanged glances and then began to laugh heartily at some unspoken jest.

Soon after leaving the village the road widened a little and on the right-hand side was bordered by a high wall of the local stone, worn and aged, as if it had been standing for a very long time. Behind it grew a thick belt of tall trees that threw long, dappled shadows across the lane. The noise of the engine altered as the rider changed gear to climb the long, steep hill and then quietened as it reached the Lodge gates. They were, as the old man had said, quite unmistakable—tall stone pillars surmounted by heraldic rampant lions each holding a shield in its claws, the armorial bearings somewhat worn by time, but the lions still proud and defiant, fiercely guarding the entrance.

Pandora Smith lifted the vizor of the helmet again and smiled to herself a little grimly as she looked at them; they were as defunct and out of date as the whole concept of land ownership by inheritance that they represented. Just because some medieval warlord had wrested the land from the local peasants by sword and torture way back in history, that shouldn't give his heirs the right to keep it now, she thought angrily. She turned off the engine and then heaved the heavy bike on to its rest. There were wide, beautifully wrought iron gates between the pillars, again with the heraldic lions picked out in gold, fine examples of the skills of the blacksmith who had made them in—what?—the early seventeenth century, she guessed. Walking across to the gates, Pandora put out a hand to touch them, capable of admiring the genius that had gone into designing and making such works of art even though she loathed the establishment of wealth and privilege that had caused them to be made.

Behind the gates, on the left-hand side of the drive, there was a small one-storeyed lodge house, again built of Cotswold stone, and ornamented by an unusual turret on the wall nearest the gates, which was higher than the house and provided a small upper room that looked out over the lane. The Lodge looked empty and deserted, the neatly laid-out garden round it slightly neglected, and when Pandora called out no one came in answer to her shout. She shrugged and turned her attention to the gates, finding that they were not locked, but fastened by bolts lowered into holes in the ground on the inside. It was something of a struggle, but by putting both arms through the ironwork Pandora was able to raise one of the handles and lift the bolt free of the ground, the gate swinging open on well-oiled hinges. After wheeling the motorbike through, she carefully shut the gate behind her and then sat astride the saddle and rode on.

The drive continued through the woodland for some way before it thinned out just as the drive swung to the right. Pandora came out of the shadow of the trees into the sunlight, then stopped the bike abruptly, sitting astride it and just staring at the view before her. The ground was open now; rolling green parkland with occasional stands of high oaks and elms casting long shadows on the grass, but the dominant feature was a large lake, its waters shimmering in the sunlight, fed by a small river that cascaded over an outcrop of rock at one end, forming an irregular waterfall. At the other end of the lake, where the water was more placid and in places hidden by the spread of white and yellow-flowered lily pads, there was a white Palladian-style summerhouse, its architecture matching that of a smaller, pagoda-like structure that Pandora could just make out among the trees on a small island nearer the left-hand end of the lake. For a while she looked at the lake, then slowly, almost reluctantly, lifted her eyes to gaze at the original of the house that was mirrored in its waters.

It stood on an eminence above the lake, set among green lawns, and standing as proud and defiant as the lions that guarded it. A magnificent building in the shape of an H, with an elongated central bar, three storeys high, the angles and chimneys of the roof hidden behind an Italian balustrade. Wide shallow steps curved gracefully up to the pedimented and pilastered entrance, set in the centre of the long side of the house, but its exact symmetry of architecture was softened by the texture of the stone and by the creeper which climbed irregularly halfway up the building at one end. An early seventeenth-century house, built at the height of the Restoration period, its beauty and grandeur held Pandora spellbound for quite some time as she feasted her eyes on it. Almost she was afraid to look away, for the house was so beautiful she felt that it must be a mirage, a fairytale palace, and if she closed her eyes it would disappear. But at length she deliberately shut her eyes, held them tightly closed while she counted to ten and then laughed at herself for being so fanciful when she opened them and the house was still there, exactly as it had been for over three hundred years. She gave a long sigh, acknowledging that wealth had at least produced something worthwhile in this magnificent building, but then became angry again when she remembered that the house and the hundreds of acres of land around it were owned by just one man, and that ordinary people were debarred from even seeing it. For this was no stately home, complete with safari park or some other gimmick, its doors thrown open to attract the public; Abbots Arbory was completely private—and determined to stay that way.

It was several minutes before Pandora continued on along the drive, following its wide curve down towards the lake and the house beyond. She accelerated the powerful engine, going fast through the parkland, only checking in startled surprise when a herd of deer suddenly shot across the road in front of her and headed for the nearest patch of trees. The shock of seeing them appear in front of her made her lose her grip on the handlebar for a moment and the machine backfired noisily, the sound exploding like gunfire in the still air, and making the terrified deer run even faster for the safety and shelter of the trees.

Pandora recovered control of the bike easily enough and continued on her way more cautiously, ready now for any other animals that might be roaming loose in the park. Further on there were some more deer, but these, already nervous from the noise of the backfire, galloped well out of the way before she got near them, and the only other animals she saw were several horses in a paddock nearer to the house, but these seemed to be securely fenced in. After about half a mile she came to a cattle grid across the road, presumably designed to keep the deer out of the grounds surrounding the house and away from the lake, as was the long ditch of a ha-ha which reached out across the parkland on either side of the grid. Pandora took the grid slowly and carefully, then opened the throttle as she headed for the Palladian bridge, its three arches straddling the end of the lake where the river ran out of it and meandered away in lazy S's across the greenness of the park.

Across to the left, on the other side of the lake nearest the house, she saw another road, and on it a vehicle, a Range Rover by the look of it, also travelling towards the bridge, but approaching it from the other side. It was travelling fast, as if the driver was in a tearing hurry, and Pandora slowed, giving it time to get across the narrow bridge before her, as there didn't seem to be enough room for them to pass between the bridge's ornamented parapets at the same time. But to her surprise the Range Rover, instead of turning to cross the bridge, drove right across the end of it, completely blocking the road.

Pandora carried on across the bridge and came to a stop a few yards from the other vehicle, looking at it in some bewilderment. A man got out and strode towards her, a sporting gun under his arm and a pair of dogs at his heels.

'What the hell do you think you're doing here?' the man demanded furiously as he came up to her.

Pandora's mouth fell open in astonishment, but before she could even begin to form a reply, he added angrily, 'Can't you read? These grounds are private—there's a notice at every entrance telling you so. Now clear out, before I have you arrested for trespassing!'

He glared at her thunderously, a tall, broad-shouldered man who looked quite capable of throwing her out personally, and who would enjoy doing it too, given half a chance.

Pandora started to get off the bike. 'Look, I'm not doing any harm. I came to . . .'

'No harm? Then what the hell do you call riding that monstrosity through the park and scaring the deer? I heard the noise of it over a mile away. You yobbos are all the same. You see a straight piece of road and you think you can practise your ton-up stunts on it no matter who it belongs to. Well, you're not going to do it at Arbory. You can just turn round and get that thing out of here. *Now!*' he added curtly, his dark brows drawing into a menacing frown.

Pandora stared back at him indignantly through the tinted visor. It was evident that the man took her for a youth, one of the fraternity of young men and boys who thundered through the countryside on their motor-bikes and turned any available field into a race-track in their search for high-speed kicks. Well, Pandora en-joyed the thrills of speed-riding as much as any of them, but she certainly wasn't a boy, although she realised that it was easy enough to mistake her for one in her leather gear.

Hastily she sought to correct him. Getting off the bike and pulling it on its rest, she turned towards her accuser and lifted her hands to take off her helmet. 'You've got it all wrong. I only came here to . . .'

Her voice died away and she stood frozen as she found herself looking into the muzzle of his gun.

'You heard what I said. Clear out! If you're not out of here in five minutes I'll turn the dogs on you!'

Pandora's hands dropped loosely to her sides as she stared at the gun in appalled horror. Slowly her eyes lifted to the man's face and she saw a gleam of triumph in his eyes as he saw the frightened way she reacted. And then, suddenly, she was angry, gloriously, uncar-ingly angry. She drew her tall, slim figure in the tight-fitting trousers and high boots to its full height and turned to face her assailant.

'You coward!' Even muffled as it was by the visor her

voice carried to him quite clearly and he stiffened in surprise. 'Hiding behind your gun and your dogs!' she went on furiously. 'Why, I bet without them you'd run a mile rather than face up to me. You bloated capitalists are all the same,' she added, mimicking his earlier remark. 'You get a preconceived idea about anyone who's the slightest bit different from you and nothing and no one will ever change it—especially if you think there's the slightest danger of upsetting the status quo. Of losing even the minutest fraction of the privileged way you live! As far as you're concerned everyone who looks or acts a little differently to you has to be regarded as the enemy. You didn't even ask me what I wanted here before you started throwing your weight around.' She paused for breath. 'Why, you're nothing but a—but an ill-mannered pig—and a cowardly one at that!' she added for good measure.

The frown had left the man's face, but instead his eyes had narrowed and his mouth set into a thin, cold line, and somehow this was far more menacing than his former anger. With a mere lift of his hand the dogs moved back to the Range Rover and sat down beside it. 'Stay,' he commanded. Then he put the gun on the ground.

Deliberately he crossed the few feet of space that separated them and looked down at her, his face still taut with barely suppressed fury.

'Now,' he said through gritted teeth, 'I'm without my gun or the dogs. So *what* was it you called me?'

Pandora blinked and lifted her head to look at him. She had to lift it an awfully long way. The man towered over her, and she was tall herself. He must be well over six feet—although right now it seemed more like eight feet at least. He was broad, too; she could see the powerful set of his shoulders even under the tweed hacking jacket that he wore, and he looked as if he kept himself in trim; there was no bulge round his middle, no softness of high-living in the lean, hard face that stared down at her with such cold disdain. She took a swift glance down at his hands that had balled into tight fists and decided that she'd definitely gone too far and the time had come to get out—fast. She took a hasty step backwards.

'Er . . . I think I'd better be going.'

'What—already?' He followed her, coming up close again. 'Don't tell me you're afraid,' he added sneeringly.

Pandora took a quick look behind her as she backed away from him; the bike was only a foot or so away and she hastily grabbed the handlebars and started to swing her leg over.

But before she could do so her assailant reached out and grabbed the lapels of her jacket, yanking her towards him so that his face was only a few inches above her as he glared down at her through the visor.

'You young punk!' he said forcefully. 'Nobody calls me a coward and gets away with it. Do you understand? Nobody!' He began to shake her, so hard that her teeth rattled and her head banged against the inside of the helmet.

'Stop it! Let me go!' She put up her hands to try and stop him, but she might as well have tried to bend an iron bar.

Suddenly he pushed her away from him so that she lost her balance and fell sprawling on to the ground. He looked down at her disgustedly. 'You chicken-livered young thug! The only time you've got any guts is when you've a mob of your mates behind you—or in

front of you,' he added with a sneer. 'Now get out of
here before I really lose my temper. And tell the rest of
your Hell's Angels pack that they'll get the same treatment if I catch any of them here again.'

Pandora didn't wait for a second invitation. She
picked herself up as fast as she could and ran to the
bike, fumbling in her nervous hurry to start it so that it
stalled once before she got the engine going properly.
She took one last, frightened glance over her shoulder
at the man, the expression of cold disgust still on his
face, and then sped back up the drive the way she had
come.

He followed her in the Range Rover, of course. To
make sure she didn't frighten a rabbit or crush a few
blades of grass, presumably, Pandora thought resentfully as she turned her head and saw him driving down
close behind her. She had a few nasty moments at the
gate when she had to get off the bike and open it, but
apart from getting out to watch the man made no
attempt to either help or hinder her, even though he
saw her struggling with the bolt that seemed heavier
than ever now. At last she had the gate open and
wheeled the bike through. She turned back to close the
gate again, but the man had walked over and clanged it
shut behind her. He stood looking at her through the
ornate ironwork, waiting for her to go. Pandora suddenly felt a great rush of relief, as if she had just been
let out of a prison and he was the jailor on the other
side of the bars, watching her. Her chin came up and
she tossed her head defiantly; it was he who was in the
prison still, a prison of his own making with bars that
he had set round himself, the bars being the strict dis-
tinctions of class and wealth that separated him from
ordinary people.

He continued to watch her contemptuously until she was out of sight, but even then Pandora could feel a prickly sensation in her back as if his cold grey eyes were still boring into it. She went back the way she had come, down into the village of Arbory Magna. The two men were still sitting outside the pub and laughed openly when they saw her reappear. Pandora smiled sourly; evidently they had known full well what kind of reception she would receive. She rode on a few yards further into the village and stopped at a small, bow-windowed shop with 'POST OFFICE' written on the hoarding and a bright red telephone box outside.

Getting off the bike, Pandora reached up to take off her helmet, her long mane of tawny hair swirling round her shoulders as she shook her head to free it. The laughter of the men across the road at the pub stopped abruptly, and Pandora turned to see them staring at her in open-mouthed astonishment. She lifted a hand in derisive acknowledgement and went into the phone box. There were several numbers listed under Abbot's Arbory in the local directory: house, Estate Manager, East Lodge, West Lodge; even a big industrial concern didn't have that many lines, Pandora thought with increasing resentment. Out of curiosity she looked under Arbory, but although there were four entries with that surname, none of them was for Sir James Arbory, the proud owner of Abbot's Arbory, who had thrown her off his land in such a ruthless and high-handed manner. The sudden thought occurred to her that perhaps it hadn't been the owner, it might have been the Estate Manager. But she dismissed the idea almost at once; an employee of whatever rank would never have treated her with such arrogant contempt and ruthlessness.

Picking up the receiver, Pandora put a tenpenny piece

ready in the slot and dialled the number given for the house. The phone rang a few times and then a man's voice, beautifully modulated and in impeccable English, said, 'Abbot's Arbory. Mr Richardson speaking.'

Pandora grinned at the plummy accent, pushed the coin into the slot and answered cheerfully, 'Hallo, Uncle Charlie. It's me.'

'Pandora!' The word came out as a gasp of astonishment. 'Where are you?'

'Here, Uncle Charlie. In Arbory Magna.'

'What?' Charles Richardson's voice had a strange, strangled sort of note. 'I thought you were going to France to pick grapes this summer.'

'No, Uncle Charlie,' Pandora answered patiently, 'that was last year. This year I was going to pick peaches in Spain.'

'I don't care where it was,' he returned explosively. 'Just tell me why you aren't there.'

'There was a big storm and most of the crop on the farm we were going to got ruined, so they didn't need so many people,' Pandora explained. 'And then the girl I was going with was offered a job at a hotel in the West Indies, and obviously she couldn't turn it down.'

'Couldn't you go with her?' her uncle asked hopefully.

'No, Uncle Charlie, it was only for one. So here I am.'

'What do you mean—here you are?' he asked warily.

Brightly Pandora answered, 'I mean that I've come to stay with you for the summer, Uncle Charlie.'

'Stay with me?' he gasped, a distinct note of terror in his voice. 'But you can't stay here. You must go back to the college. Yes, that's it—you must stay in college during the vacation and study for your exams. It will do you good to be able to work without any distractions from the other students,' he added, growing increasingly enamoured of the idea.

Pandora let him go on for a while and then interrupted. 'It's no good, Uncle Charlie, the college is closed and I'm broke.'

'What about your allowance?'

'I spent it.'

'Well, you could get a job somewhere, couldn't you?' he asked with a note of despair in his voice.

'Uncle Charlie, *I have nowhere to live.*'

'A live-in job—at a hotel or something,' he urged, with a last desperate try.

Pandora was silent for a long moment, then said in a small voice, 'All right, Uncle Charlie. I realise you don't want me. Even though when Mother died you promised that you'd look after me.' She stifled a sob. 'You're all I've got left, Uncle. I thought I could come to you for help.' She sniffed bravely. 'But I—I'll just have to manage on my own. I'll just walk the streets until . . .'

'Walk the streets!' he exploded. 'My God, girl, do you know what you're saying?'

'Why, only that I'll have to go back to London and walk around until I find someone who'll take me in,' Pandora answered innocently.

Her uncle's voice faded into a strangled gasp of horror and it was several seconds before he recovered sufficiently to say weakly, 'You—you can't do that. I suppose you'd better come here while I sort something out for you. I might be able to get you a job with some people I used to be in service with who've now opened a guesthouse on the coast. But it's only for a couple of days, mind,' he added warningly. 'You can't stay longer than that.'

'No, Uncle Charlie,' Pandora agreed meekly. 'I quite understand. It's very kind of you, Uncle Charlie.'

'And stop calling me that,' he said in exasperation. 'You know I dislike it excessively.'

'Of course. I'm very sorry, Uncle Charlie,' Pandora agreed, her hand coming up to her mouth to stifle a giggle, picturing her rather pompous uncle in his black butler's suit, and the devastating effect her phone call would have on him. But she had known that she would get her own way; she always did, ever since the death of her mother when she was twelve and he had become her legal guardian.

Now he sighed heavily and said, 'You'd better come up to the house. You go through the village and up the hill to ...'

Pandora coughed. 'I don't think that would be a good idea, Uncl ... hmm. You see, I already tried to come to the house, but I ... well, sort of got thrown out.'

'You got what?' he demanded.

'Thrown out. By a man with a gun and couple of dogs,' Pandora supplied helpfully.

'What did he look like?'

'Oh, very tall, dark, and arrogant.'

Her uncle had no difficulty in recognising the description. 'Dear God, what have I done to deserve this? That was Sir James himself!'

'Yes, I rather thought it might be.'

'But why did he throw you out? Didn't you tell him you were coming to visit me?'

'Well, I didn't really have a chance,' Pandora explained. 'You see, he sort of took exception to my motorbike and he ...'

'Motorbike? You didn't drive up here on that thing,

did you?' A sound suspiciously like a moan came over the line. 'He'll never let you stay here now.'

'But does he have to know?'

But her words were drowned by her uncle's mournful wail. 'I knew it was too good to last! I just get myself settled in a decent place and get things running exactly as I like them and you come along and lose me my job—again!'

'Uncle Charlie, it really wasn't my fault I watered all those prize orchids with weedkiller at your last place. The watering can wasn't marked; it could have happened to anyone,' Pandora pleaded, genuinely sorry for her uncle's distress. 'And it *was* two years ago. Look,' she said persuasively, 'Abbot's Arbory is a huge place. If you sneaked me in by a side entrance or something, your boss wouldn't even know I was there. Why, I bet you could hide a dozen people in the attics alone and no one would ever find them.'

It took a lot of persuasion and wheedling, but at last Pandora got her uncle to agree to let her stay at Abbot's Arbory, although she had to make a great many promises, all of which he seemed to think vitally necessary if he was going to keep his job. Personally Pandora thought that if Sir James Arbory was such a tyrant—as her own brief clash with him proved—then she would be doing Uncle Charlie a favour by getting him the sack. But he knew his own business best, so she shrugged and dutifully promised not to approach the house again but to wait until after dark when he would come to fetch her and slip her in by the back door. Although Uncle Charlie didn't put it quite like that, of course, he described it as 'unobtrusively escorting you to the tradesmen's entrance'.

With several hours to kill, Pandora rode into the

nearest town and did some envious window-shopping for a while, then found herself walking past the local library and wandered in to read the daily paper and browse through the glossy fashion magazines, all of which were always beyond her allowance. By the time she had paid her rent and bought books and food—in that order—there was rarely any left for luxuries like fashion magazines, or much in the way of clothes at all for that matter. After an hour or so she turned to leave the library, but she had to go through the reference section and her eye was caught by the massive volume of *Burke's Peerage*. An idea occurred to her and she took the book from the shelf and across to a table. Flicking over the first few pages in the A's, she ran her finger over the columns and stopped at the one she wanted. It read:

'Sir James Tristan Wyndham Arbory, 12th Bt., of Abbot's Arbory, Arbory Magna, Oxon. b. 17th Dec. 1945, succeeded his father. Educ. Eton and Oriel College, Oxford. Clubs: Whites, Carlton. Lineage: descended from Sir Edward Arbory, knighted 1417' which was followed by a long line of descendants.

Pandora did a rapid mental calculation; so that made him thirty-five, and there was no mention of a wife or children, so that meant he was still a bachelor.

She slammed the huge book shut suddenly, annoyed that she had let her curiosity get the better of her. What did it matter to her who or what the owner of Abbot's Arbory was? As far as she was concerned he was just a capitalist leech who was feeding off the backs of the workers. Why, he must have a dozen servants, besides Uncle Charlie, to run a place that size. The whole system was shockingly unfair, and the sooner it was changed the better.

She drove back to Arbory Magna in the cool of the evening, the scent of the hedgerows strong on the light breeze, and waited at a table outside the pub for her uncle to turn up. He didn't come until it was quite dark, trudging purposefully up the lane in the beautifully pressed dark trousers and blazer that he considered to be the correct casual wear for a man in his position. Pandora smiled to herself; much as she loved her only relative, she just had to admit that he was awfully pompous.

He came up to her with a stern frown on his face, but this melted as Pandora jumped up impulsively to give him a hug and plant a kiss on his cheek. He tut-tutted a bit and tried to look askance, but was secretly not displeased at her show of affection.

'Really, child,' he remonstrated, 'what if someone I knew saw us? What would they think?'

Pandora opéned her eyes wide. 'I don't know, Uncle. What would they think?'

As usual he was flummoxed for an answer, as Pandora knew he would be. It was one of Uncle Charlie's most endearing traits that he lived in a world way back in the nineteenth century, when all unmarried girls were pure as the driven snow. It made Pandora sigh with exasperation at times, but she often traded on it shamelessly to her own advantage.

'Well, hmm, never mind. Come along. We'd better be on our way.'

Obediently Pandora picked up her helmet and gloves. 'You can ride pillion, Uncle Charlie.'

He immediately looked affronted. 'Certainly not! I wouldn't be seen dead on that contraption. We'll walk and you'll have to push it.'

'But it's over a mile,' Pandora objected.

'Yes, and another mile or so after we reach the gates,' her uncle added, not without a certain satisfaction. 'You should have thought of that before you came here on it. Why you couldn't come by train like any other normal person, I don't know.'

He rabbited on in much the same vein for nearly half a mile while Pandora pushed the bike along beside him, with only an occasional grunt which he could take whichever way he liked. As the hill climbed more steeply she began to pant with exertion, concentrating all her efforts on pushing the heavy bike, but then her uncle lent a grudging hand, then two hands, until they arrived at the lodge gates and rested in a panting but companionable silence.

Pandora had expected them to go through the gates, but Charles Richardson led her on for another couple of hundred yards to another smaller and less ornate gate which he unlocked and which led through trees round to the back of the great house; a way for tradesmen's vehicles which was hidden from the windows of the house or anyone strolling in the park. When they got near the outbuildings he motioned her to silence and led the way almost stealthily to an old coach-house that looked as if it hadn't been used for quite some time.

'You can hide the bike in here,' he said in a low, hissing whisper, at the same time looking furtively over his shoulder.

'Oh, really, Uncle Charlie,' Pandora said in exasperation. 'Anyone would think we were committing a crime!'

He flapped his hands to shush her. 'Quiet! Sir James often takes a stroll in the evening; he might hear us.'

Pandora sighed, but quietly removed her belongings from the leather panniers on the bike and followed him

to a side door of the house. It led to a long, plain corridor with brown-varnished doors opening off at either
side and at the end of it a flight of uncarpeted steps
leading upwards, but her uncle stopped at a door just
before the end and opened it.

'Here you are,' he said in a rather more confident
tone. 'You can have this room. It's quite clean and
aired because we had a maid who left only recently. She
only stayed a few weeks—said she couldn't stand being
stuck in the country.' He sniffed disparagingly. 'No sta-
mina in today's younger generation. *And* the agency
haven't found us a replacement yet. Still, that's neither
here nor there.' He looked at her consideringly, seeing
her in a good light for the first time. 'You're looking
thin,' he remarked, his eyes running reprovingly over
her tall slim figure. 'I don't suppose you bother to cook
yourself proper meals—just live on convenience foods
in that college of yours.'

'Never mind, Uncle Charlie,' Pandora said bracingly.
'While I'm here you can fatten me up.'

'Humph!' He went to draw the curtains across the
window for her. 'And why you find it necessary to wear
that ridiculous outfit, I fail to see.'

'But it's ideal for the motorbike. I got the leathers
cheaply from a student who didn't need them any
more.'

'Oh? Did he buy a car instead?'

'No. He just crashed his bike and broke both his
legs,' Pandora returned calmly.

Her uncle raised his eyes to heaven. 'Well, I hope
you've got some more respectable clothes to wear.'

'Of course I have. I've got jeans and tee-shirts . . .'

His face paled and he held up a hand to stop her.
'Don't tell me any more, I don't want to know. When
you're ready come down to the kitchen and I'll get

you some food. You go back down this corridor, turn left at the end and go through the scullery to the kitchen.'

He left her alone and Pandora looked round the room. It was, as he had said, clean, and to her surprise it was quite amply if plainly furnished with a vanity unit in one corner, a square of grey carpet, a single bed with a navy cover that matched the curtains, and a varnished wardrobe and dressing table. There was also an armchair, again upholstered in navy and which Pandora sank into gratefully while she pulled off her boots; they had never been intended for walking, let alone that long trek from the village. When she went to hang the few clothes she had brought with her in the wardrobe she found two black dresses, two dark grey skirts and cardigans, and two white blouses, all encased in polythene bags, hanging there, obviously freshly back from the cleaners after the maid had left. Pandora looked at the cut of the garments and grimaced; no wonder the girl had left if she had been expected to wear that outdated gear, it was at least two decades behind the times.

Pandora washed and then, bearing in mind Uncle Charlie's strictures, changed into her most conservative pair of jeans, without any patches or badges sewn on, and a tee-shirt that, although bright red, merely had 'I'M INTO THE EIGHTIES' written across the chest and which she hoped wouldn't offend his sensibilities too much.

Apart from a shudder when he saw her, her uncle carefully refrained from comment, merely placing a bowl of soup and a dish of rolls in front of her, followed by a large ham omelette. Pandora ate hungrily while he sat and watched her morosely. Afterwards she sat back and wiped her lips on a napkin. 'That was delicious. Uncle Charlie, you really are a great cook.'

He looked pleased. 'Well, I will admit that I can turn

out a good omelette.'

'But you don't have to cook for this Sir James, do you? Surely he has a professional chef?'

'He does when there are guests staying, but when he's alone here the housekeeper usually does the meals.'

'The housekeeper? Does she live in the house too?'

'Yes, but she's away at the moment looking after her mother who's just had an operation.'

'Do any other staff live in?'

'Not in the house itself now the maid's left. There's a groom and a stableboy who live near the stableyard, and various gamekeepers and gardeners who live in tied cottages on the estate, but there's only myself in the house at the moment.'

'And so you're doing the cooking?'

'Yes.' A frown crossed his brow. 'But he's getting a bit fed up with omelettes.'

Pandora burst into a peal of laughter and her uncle gave a wry grin and then laughed openly.

'That's better,' Pandora told him. 'You've been a crotchety old bear ever since I phoned you. I was beginning to be afraid you'd forgotten how to laugh.'

He shook his head. 'I'm sorry, child. It's just that I've really grown to like it here and I don't want to lose my place. And I'm—well, I'm getting a bit too old to keep changing jobs. I'd like to settle here if I can. That's why you must promise to stay here in the kitchen area,' he added urgently. 'Sir James wouldn't like it if he knew I'd let you stay here when he'd already turned you off.'

Pandora's heart was immediately wrung and she put out her hands to cover his. 'Don't worry, Uncle, I'll keep out of his way. After this afternoon I've no wish to run into him again, believe me. I'd rather meet a man-eating lion. Or even a woman-eating lion if it came to that!'

She went to bed shortly after and slept soundly until she was awakened early the next morning by the unusual sounds of birds singing and somewhere not too far away a cock crowing fit to wake every hen for miles around. Pandora turned over and tried to go to sleep again when she saw how early it was, but all the bird population of the Cotswolds seemed to have congregated outside her window and were pouring out their shrill welcome. Giving in to the inevitable, she got up and opened the curtains. The room looked out on to a paved yard, but beyond it, at the back of the house, there were lawns edged with banks of flowers, their bright heads glowing in the dawn sunlight, the drops of dew glistening like diamonds on the velvet petals and leaves.

Pandora turned back into the room and looked at the cream walls and drab carpet and curtains. What this room needed was colour—lots of it. It needed to be filled with flowers. Now, this minute! Impulsively she turned and ran out of the room and down the corridor to the outside door just as she was: barefooted, her long tawny hair falling free, and dressed just in a long, creamy-white full-skirted Victorian-style nightdress, its long sleeves gathered at the wrists.

The air struck cold as she opened the outer door, but she ran on heedlessly across the yard and down some steps to the lawn. The grass was wet under her feet, the morning mist not yet lifted by the sun, so that she felt as if she was running through a cloud. She laughed with delight as the mist swirled around her, happy to be in the country, to be free of work and studying for a while, to be able to relax and to live only for this beautiful morning. Her laughter rang out through the still air as she danced across the grass, twirling round and round so that her skirts belled out around her legs. She bent to bury her head in a mass of roses, drinking in their heady scent, and when some petals came loose in her hands, threw them up into the air and watched entranced as they drifted in the dappled sunlight, the breeze catching them and prolonging their flight in dizzy circles before they came gently down to rest. She reached up to where the lilac blossom hung heavy on the bough, deep mauve and shiny virgin white, and gasped and laughed with delight as the branches showered her with dewdrops. She filled her arms with heavenly-scented carnations, with big white daisies, and irises of every shade, yellow and blue and white and salmon.

She flitted from flower to flower like an exotic butterfly, quite a way from the house, and it was only when her arms were so full that she couldn't hold any more that she turned and ran happily back. Pushing the outer door open with her shoulder, she heard a noise in the kitchen and ran towards it, eager to show Uncle Charlie her treasure trove and demand a dozen vases to put them all in. She burst through the kitchen door and turned towards her uncle, green eyes alight with eagerness, her hair a wind-blown tangle. She began to say 'Uncle——' but then stopped with her mouth wide open, frozen by surprise and alarm.

Her uncle wasn't alone in the kitchen. Sitting negligently on the edge of the table, a mug of coffee in his hands, was the owner of Abbot's Arbory, the lord of the manor, and most definitely the man who had ejected her so violently only yesterday, Sir James Arbory!

CHAPTER TWO

THERE was an almighty crash as Charles Richardson dropped the brown earthenware teapot he was holding and it shattered on the stone floor. Pandora gulped, took one look at her uncle's agonised features, and hastily backed towards the door.

'No, don't go.' The tone was as imperative as the order.

She hesitated, giving another beseeching look towards her relative, but he seemed to be as frozen as she had been. Reluctantly Pandora turned to look at Sir James.

Today he was wearing tan riding breeches and a dark brown riding coat, his feet shod in beautifully polished leather boots. A crop and a brown velvet riding hat were nearby on the table. Slowly Pandora lifted her eyes to his face, expecting to see there the frown of anger that he had displayed the previous day, but to her surprise he didn't seem to be angry at all, in fact there was a curl of amusement on his thin, rather sardonic lips, and his eyes when they ran over her held a gleam of appreciation.

Pandora suddenly became acutely aware that she was wearing only her nightdress, that the hem of it was wet, and clinging to her legs.

Sir James put down his cup and standing up, took a couple of steps towards her. 'Good morning. I don't believe we've met. I'm James Arbory.'

He waited, obviously expecting her to introduce herself. Pandora flashed another glance at her uncle, but he still seemed to be struck dumb. She made a strangled sort of choking sound, then shrugged helplessly and opened her mouth to tell him who she was.

But her uncle came to sudden life and interjected hastily, 'She's from London, sir.'

His employer nodded. 'From the domestic agency—so I gathered. It's about time they sent a replacement for the last maid.'

Uncle Charlie looked stunned and Pandora had to stifle a hasty laugh. Dazedly he said, 'Yes, sir. Quite so.'

Sir James looked at her again and said, 'But you haven't told me your name.'

'It's Smith, sir,' her uncle put in before she could speak. He frowned at her mightily. 'But she might just as well go straight back to London without waiting for a month's trial; it's quite obvious that anyone who goes wandering round the gardens in her night attire—*and* picking some of your best blooms—is entirely unsuitable for such an establishment as this. I'll see that she leaves straight away. Go to your room at once, girl, and pack your things,' he ordered dismissively.

Pandora turned to leave, but Sir James' next words halted her in her tracks. 'On the contrary, I think it might make a pleasant change to have so conscientious a maid that she ran out to pick flowers for the house while the dew was still on them. That's the best time to pick flowers, of course. But you knew that, didn't you?' he remarked as he came to take the huge bouquet from her arms and pass them to her uncle.

There was mockery in his voice and in his eyes as he said it. That, and something else as he looked down at her. Pandora followed his gaze and saw that the dew from the flowers had wet her nightdress, clearly revealing the outline of her breasts beneath. Angrily she moved so that the material no longer clung, a flash of fire in her green eyes. So that was the kind of man he was, was he? There had been too many men in the past who had looked at her in just that way for her to fail to recognise it now.

'But we can't call you Smith,' he was saying. 'What's your first name?'

She opened her mouth to speak, but her uncle quickly crossed over to them and said hastily, 'It's Dora, sir. Dora Smith.' Pandora cringed inwardly but made no objection.

There was hidden laughter in his employer's face as he said, 'Well, Dora Smith, from London, welcome to Abbot's Arbory. It's going to be *very* interesting having you here.'

Pandora looked into his cool grey eyes, alight with amusement, and wondered whether that last remark had been intended as a double entendre. Well, whether it was or not, one thing was for sure—she disliked Sir High-and-Mighty Arbory excessively and it would give her great pleasure to wipe that leering grin off his face. An idea came to her and her eyes lit with mischief as she opened her mouth, and in a broad nasal Cockney accent said, 'Ooh, ta ever so. I ain't 'arf pleased to be 'ere, an' all.'

He physically flinched. She could see the shudder pass through his face, even though he concealed it well, and she felt an inner glow of satisfaction which she was careful not to let show, merely looking up at him in what she hoped was a gormless manner. Beside her, Uncle Charlie made a despairing, choking noise, but Pandora carefully avoided looking at him in case she gave anything away.

'Yes, well—er . . .' Sir James seemed to be at a loss

for words. 'As Mr Richardson has said, you'd better go
and get changed. You can put the flowers in water
later.'

Pandora bestowed a bland smile on them both.
'Right you are then, ducks. Shan't be more than 'arf a
mo.'

She escaped to her room and collapsed against the
closed door, stifling her laughter with her hand. Even if
she was kicked out tomorrow it would have been worth
it just to see the expression on their faces when she had
called Sir James Tristan Wyndham Arbory, Bart,
ducks. It was hard to tell who had been the more appalled, Sir James or her uncle. Still chuckling, she began
to dress, and going to the wardrobe looked at the
maid's uniforms hanging there. Presumably the dresses
were worn in the evening and the skirts and blouses for
housework during the day. How ridiculous when jeans
and sweaters were so much more practical. After putting
on the clothes, Pandora came to the conclusion that the
previous maid must have been short and plump; the
skirt was too big round the waist and barely reached to
her knees. She found a safety pin and was able to put a
big tuck in the waist, but there was nothing she could
do about the length. The blouse and cardigan too were
baggy, although the sleeves were too short. There didn't
seem to be any sort of cap to wear with the uniform,
thank goodness, but she supposed she'd have to do
something with her hair; she couldn't imagine Uncle
Charlie approving of it being loose. So she carefully
scraped it back off her face and plaited it into a long
braid, then coiled it round her head.

When she had finished Pandora looked at herself in
the mirror and laughed aloud. She looked terrible! Like
a caricature from a theatrical farce. Nothing could

hide the fine bone structure of her face, the beauty of
her long-lashed green eyes, but without make-up, her
hair in this ugly uncomplimentary style, and with the
dowdy, badly-fitting clothes *and* that ghastly Cockney
accent, then she defied even Sir James to find her attractive. But that he had on first seeing her, Pandora
was sure; the arrested look on his face had been unmistakable. The green eyes looking back at her from the
mirror darkened with annoyance. It would be interesting to see whether Sir James Arbory would lower his
standards or whether he would be too fastidious to contemplate making amorous advances to an employee,
and especially to one who was obviously uneducated,
vulgar and common at that. Her eyes lit up with mischief at the game she was about to play. She did feel a
pang of regret that her uncle would have to play a help-
less part in it, but for Sir James she felt no sympathy at
all; it served him right for throwing her out so ruth-
lessly, and for being the arrogant snob that he was.

Before going back to the kitchen, she practised a few
inane grins and silly, simpering giggles in the mirror
until she was sure she could turn them on at will. It
would never do to let her new boss know that there was
a brain behind the caricature. This was a game that,
once started, had to go on until he just couldn't stand
having her around any longer. And judging from her
appearance that would be sooner rather than later.

When she went back to the kitchen she found her
uncle alone. A pained expression crossed his face when
he saw her, then he sighed resignedly.

'Here, you'd better sit down and have some breakfast.'

He put two plates of scrambled eggs down on the
table and sat down opposite her. Opening the daily

paper, he folded it and perused the columns in a
gloomy silence. After a couple of minutes Pandora
peered over at the paper and saw that he was studying
the Situations Vacant—Domestic columns.

'Are you trying to find me a job?' she asked him.

He lifted his head and looked at her morosely. 'No,
I'm trying to find myself one.'

Pandora stared. 'Has he fired you?'

'No, not yet. But he will. Just as soon as the next
disaster happens and he finds out you're my niece.'

'But what makes you think something terrible is
going to happen?' Pandora protested.

'It's bound to. You're a walking disaster area—
always have been,' he answered, his voice heavy with
gloomy foreboding. 'I don't know why he even contemplated keeping you on after the exhibition you made of
yourself this morning. Fancy coming into the kitchen
like that!'

'I didn't know he was in here,' Pandora objected.

Her uncle frowned. 'It doesn't matter who was in
here—you shouldn't have come in like that. What on
earth possessed you to go out picking flowers—and in
your nightdress too? Couldn't you at least have got
dressed first?'

Pandora looked surprised. 'It never occurred to me.
The sun was shining, I saw the flowers, so I just went
out and picked them.'

He studied her face for a while, then set down his cup
resignedly. 'It's no use; I've tried and tried, but I shall
never understand you. Why is it you can't behave like
an ordinary human being and think before you do
things instead of acting on impulse all the time, I shall
never know. Why, I remember when you were only
about ten, you . . .'

He began to warm to his theme and Pandora decided that she had better interrupt before he really got going; unfortunately he had a good memory, and she had the uneasy feeling that she had committed enough misdemeanours in the past for him to go on for hours. So she said firmly, 'Why did you tell me to stay round the kitchen area when he comes down here for breakfast every day?'

The diversion worked. 'But he doesn't,' Uncle Charlie replied. 'I always serve him early morning coffee in his room at six-thirty, then he goes out riding and comes back for breakfast about nine. And I always serve that in the morning room. In the two years I've been here I've never known him to come down to the kitchen before.' He shook his head wonderingly. 'It must be fate that he should come down today of all days. There must be some malign aura about you that just draws disaster wherever you go.'

Pandora had to laugh at the woeful expression on his face, but she said sympathetically, 'Oh, come on, Uncle Charlie, it isn't as bad as that. Look on the bright side. If I do do something terrible you can always remind him that you said I wasn't suitable right at the start. And I won't tell him we're related—promise. And now you won't have to put yourself out trying to find me a job,' she added bracingly as he showed no sign of cheering up. 'In fact, it's all worked out quite well, really.'

He snorted derisively. 'Quite well! You're bound to do something terrible and get us both fired. Probably break a piece of priceless china or something.'

'No, I won't. I'll be very good, you'll see. I'll be the perfect maid,' Pandora told him optimistically.

'Oh, will you? Then will you please tell me why you found it necessary to speak to him in that terrible Cockney accent?' he demanded indignantly.

'Oh, that.' Pandora flushed guiltily. 'Well, I—I just thought I would,' she said inadequately, but adding more firmly as an idea came to her, 'You see, I thought it would help *you*.'

'Help me? How on earth could it?'

'Well, I thought that if I spoke like that all the time, he'd soon get fed up with having me around and would fire me that much sooner.'

Her uncle grunted, only slightly mollified, but said, 'It won't make any difference. People in Sir James' position don't go around talking to the maids all day! I shall be surprised if he ever bothers to speak to you again.'

'Oh, I see.'

He bent his head to his paper again, and Pandora was heartened to see that he did at least turn the pages and begin to read the news items instead. There had been no way she could tell him the real reason for adopting the phoney accent; he would have been incredibly shocked and either told her that she was completely mistaken or else insisted on clucking round her like an old hen with its last surviving chick in case any attack should be made on her virtue. Pandora grinned to herself at the old-fashioned term, but that was Uncle Charlie—a throwback to the nineteenth century.

As she finished her breakfast she wondered whether Sir James would, in fact, ever speak to her again. After a few moments' thought she decided that he probably would try to chat her up, but probably not for a few days. He would have to have time to recover from the initial shock before he ventured near her a second time. So she would have to think of something that would really put him off her. She chuckled, imagining several ways she could do it, and her uncle looked up from his paper suspiciously.

'Now what are you planning?'

Pandora smiled back at him serenely. 'Nothing, Uncle, nothing at all for you to worry about.'

'Oh, no!' he groaned. 'When you say something like that I start worrying most of all.'

But after breakfast he recovered sufficiently to show her where everything was kept in the kitchen and set her to cleaning out some cupboards while he prepared his master's breakfast. Pandora was amused to see that eggs played a large part in it and even felt a small twinge of sympathy for Sir James if he had to live on her uncle's cooking for very long. It seemed that he was going out during the course of the morning, so later on Uncle Charlie took her round the house, showing it off with as much pride as if it was his own. And Pandora had to admit that it was magnificent. It was a house that had been cared for through the centuries, with every generation adding to the treasure of furniture, porcelain and paintings that adorned every room. Other stately homes open to the public that Pandora had visited had had a museumlike atmosphere, a smell of mustiness from old, decaying books and hangings, but there was none of that here; the rooms smelt fresh and clean, the curtains looked comparatively new and there were no chairs with the stuffing showing because the last faded and tatty remnants of the original covers had to be preserved and displayed.

They paused in the long gallery, which had several floor-to-ceiling bookcases along one wall and windows looking out across the park on the other. It must have been at least a hundred feet long with a beautifully ornate marble fireplace at each end. These were not lit and it should have been a cold place, but the sun streamed through the windows, warming it and giving life to the family portraits on the walls and the rich polished wood of the furniture. After admiring it silently for a few moments, Pandora had a nasty shock when Uncle Charlie said, 'One of your duties will be to keep this, and all the other rooms that Sir James uses every day, dusted and tidy.'

She looked at him aghast. 'Good heavens, you don't have to keep this whole place clean by yourself, do you? Or with just a maid to help you? Why, that's slave labour! You must be working all day long.'

'No, of course I don't. We have three women who come in to clean every weekday, but they only do the rough work: washing floors and paintwork, vacuum cleaning, polishing, and that sort of thing. It's up to the maid to just dust and tidy up and to prepare the guest rooms if Sir James invites anyone down for the weekend.'

'Is anyone coming this weekend?' Pandora asked, remembering that it was Saturday.

Her uncle assured her that there wasn't and then led her to a cupboard full of cleaning materials and firmly told her to get to work. 'And *please*—try not to drop anything,' he admonished her as he left.

Although Pandora found even the idea of being someone's servant repugnant, she was surprised to find that she quite enjoyed herself that day. It was fun to dust a portrait and wonder what kind of life the sitter had had here in Abbot's Arbory so long ago; would they have sat at the ornate desk to write their letters, have danced in the ballroom with its magnificent chandeliers, or sat in the armchair before the fire with all its ornate carving that made it difficult to dust? And it was a rare privilege to handle some of the delicate porcelain ornaments that adorned tables and sideboards, pieces that normally you were only allowed to stare at through glass cases in museums.

Pandora picked up one beautiful group of a richly dressed man and woman with two spaniels at their heels, the richness of their clothes glowing with life and colour, and lifted it up to look at the maker's mark underneath. As she'd thought; there were the two crossed swords, hilts downwards, which proclaimed that it had been made in the famous Meissen factory in East Germany.

'Good afternoon, Dora.'

The voice coming unexpectedly from close behind her startled her so much that she jumped and dropped the ornament. It fell headlong towards the marble-topped table on which it had been standing, but James Arbory's hand shot out and caught it only a couple of inches from the surface. Pandora let out a long breath and slowly unfroze. She smiled in relief and turned to find her new employer's eyes on her face, studying her intently. It reminded her suddenly of the game she was playing; in her gladness at not breaking the ornament she had almost forgotten and blurted out her thanks in her normal voice.

Now she said, 'Coo, blimey, you didn't 'arf make me jump, creepin' up on me like that! Gave me a proper turn, you did. You're lucky that pot didn't get broken. Still, it's only an old one, innit?'

'As you say, it's only an old one—but rather precious for all that.' He carefully replaced the group on the table and said casually, 'Are you interested in porcelain figurines?'

'In what?' Pandora frowned in perplexity.

'In figures like these.' He indicated the ornament. 'You seemed to be looking at the maker's mark on the bottom.'

'Is that what the black mark was? I thought it was sumthin' that had got stuck on and I was tryin' to rub it

orf. Cor, I'd a' been rubbin' all day, wouldn't I, ducks?'
And she giggled like a silly, simpering schoolgirl.

His dark brows drew together in a frown, a perplexed
look in his eyes, and Pandora hoped that she had fooled
him again. She would have to be careful, though; she
had had to think quickly over the porcelain mark.

His eyes left her face and ran over her, taking in the
baggy clothes. 'That uniform doesn't seem to fit you
very well.'

Pandora looked down at herself. 'No. I think that
other girl must 'ave been a bit bigger'n me.'

'*Quite* a bit bigger,' he agreed. 'You'd better tell Mr
Richardson to give you some time off next week so that
you can go into Oxford and get a uniform that fits.'

'Righty'o.'

Pandora went to turn away, but he said, 'By the way,
where were you employed before?'

Her mind raced as she turned slowly back to face
him: if she said she had been employed by a family he
would be bound to ask for a reference which she most
deffnitely couldn't supply. She thought of several other
possibilities, but decided it would be better to keep it as
near the truth as possible, so she answered, 'I worked in
a college; makin' the students' beds and cleaning out
their rooms an' that. But it was casual work. I 'ad to
find other jobs during the 'olidays, workin' in 'otels and
that. But I said t'meself, Dora me girl, I said, you've got
ter find yourself a proper job. So I went to the agency
and they sent me 'ere. They said this would be a proper
job,' she explained helpfully.

'Did they, indeed?' A glint of amusement showed in
James Arbory's lean features. 'And what about your
family, your parents; do they approve of your coming
here?'

A shadow crossed her face. 'I haven't . . .' she stopped

and said quickly, 'I ain't got no family. Me parents is dead.'

'I'm sorry.' There was a surprising gentleness in his voice. 'And you have no one else to care for you?'

Pandora hesitated, then said, 'Only me Uncle Charlie,' and added because she couldn't resist it, 'And 'e's inside at the moment.'

'Inside?' He frowned in puzzlement and then said, 'Oh. Oh, I see,' having taken the expression by its slang meaning which was that someone was in prison, as Pandora had hoped he would. Although it was literally true: her Uncle Charlie was inside at the moment— here, inside this house.

'Yes, well—I hope that you'll be happy here, Dora, and if you have any problems please don't hesitate to come to me or to Mr Richardson. Perhaps you could go along to Mr Richardson now and tell him that I won't be in to dinner.'

'In t' dinner?' Pandora looked at an ornate ormolu clock on the mantelshelf. 'But it's 'arf past four. Dinner time was hours ago.'

His mouth twisted wryly. 'Yes, well, perhaps you could just tell him that I won't be in to the evening meal, then.'

'You won't be in ter supper. Righty'o, I'll go and tell 'im right now. Ta-ra.'

She picked up her duster and keeping her face perfectly straight because there were several mirrors in the room, walked out and carefully shut the door behind her, then ran through the corridor leading to the back stairs, gurgling with laughter.

So later that evening she and Uncle Charlie dined in solitary state in the kitchen, and the butler didn't take much persuading to open a bottle of wine from his master's amply stocked cellars. Although it wasn't one of his better wines, as he hastened to point out. But whether one of the best vintages or not, it certainly mellowed him, and as Pandora had insisted on cooking the meal and she was a very good cook, the evening passed very satisfactorily.

They played chess afterwards and Pandora let her uncle win three times out of four and did it so skilfully that he thought he had genuinely beaten her, so that he was *almost* pleased that she was staying on. She told him something of the progress she was making at London University where she was studying for a degree, hoping to eventually get a job as a librarian, and Uncle Charlie in turn told her how he found life at Abbot's Arbory. He wasn't usually so loquacious and in such a good mood, so Pandora let him ramble on, although she couldn't work up much interest in the intricacies of cleaning silver or the trouble he had getting the gardeners to bring the vegetables and fruit he wanted up to the house.

'Of course it will be much better when Mrs Symons, the housekeeper, gets back. What with her being away and Jessop in hospital . . .'

'Jessop?' Pandora queried.

'He's the man who lives at the East Lodge. He's quite an elderly man, lived on the estate all his life and now just sees to the gate and does a few maintenance jobs round the house.'

'Why is he in hospital?' Pandora carefully placed her knight so that her uncle could take it with his bishop.

He snorted angrily. 'Because a crowd of motorcycling rowdies pushed their way in one night and started to race each other round the park. Jessop called the police. Two of the mares were in foal and Jessop was frightened something would happen to them, so he tried to stop the cyclists himself.' His face darkened. 'One of them knocked him down with his motorbike and he broke his leg.'

Pandora stared at him appalled. 'So that was why he was so angry with me! Why he aimed a gun at me.'

Her uncle smiled triumphantly as he took her knight. 'Who, Sir James? I'm not surprised. I've never seen him so angry as that night. He didn't know anything about it until he got back quite a few hours later, and then he insisted on going off to the hospital there and then to see how Jessop was, and then he went down to the police station and created merry hell until he was sure that every last one of the gang had been rounded up.' He took another drink of his second bottle of wine and added, 'Personally I think he would have been pleased if he could have taken the law into his own hands and taught those punks a lesson they wouldn't forget in a hurry. He could have done it too.'

Pandora remembered Sir James' broad shoulders, and the way he had squared up to her so menacingly, and shivered. 'Yes, I'm quite sure he could,' she murmured feelingly.

She played rather abstractedly after that and her uncle really did win the game, but when he proposed another she refused, saying that she was tired. She helped him to clear up and then said goodnight and went to her room. She kicked off her shoes, but instead of undressing straightaway, sat on the bed for some time gazing pensively into space, and at length she got up and changed into jeans and a sweater and quietly let herself out of the house.

A bright moon illuminated her way as she walked slowly through the gardens towards the lake and the park beyond. In the distance an owl hooted in the trees, but apart from that the night was incredibly peaceful, not even a breath of wind to disturb the leaves of the trees. The lake was silver in the moonlight, rippled now and then as a fish came to the surface. Pandora walked down to the edge, her bare feet silent on the springy grass, and stood looking out over the park for some time before she turned and looked back at the house. There was nothing dark or mysterious about the place. Even at night, when it was in complete darkness except for a single light over the entrance door, left on as a welcome for its master, the house looked warm and hospitable in the moonlight, as if she had only to say the word and the doors would open to receive her, the lights blaze out, the rooms fill with music and laughter . . .

In the distance a horse neighed, breaking her reverie. Pandora gave herself a mental shake and walked over to sit on a wooden seat that circled the massive trunk of a huge old oak tree. She tucked her feet up under her and looked musingly at the house. It seemed that she had been unjust in her first summing up of the master of Abbot's Arbory. Maybe he wasn't such a tyrant after all, if he had thought that she was yet another member of the original Hell's Angel gang who had put one of his servants in hospital. It was just her bad luck that she had happened along only a few days later and had taken the brunt of his anger. So it seemed that she would have to revise her opinion of him. But strangely she felt an odd reluctance to do so; he was rich, titled, and powerful, one of a group she despised, and it suited her that he should conform to type, to be hard and arrogant. That he should have raised hell because his old servant had been hurt meant that she could no longer fit him neatly into his pigeonhole. If it had been just his precious horses he had got het up about she could have understood; the English were notorious for the way they cared more about animals than they did about people. No, she would much rather not have known that he had a bona fide reason for threatening her; it cheapened the game she was playing somehow. But once started, of course, there was no way of going back.

She continued to sit there, deep in thought, for some time, and didn't notice the twin points of light gradually increasing in size as a car travelled towards the house, its engine running so quietly that it made no disturbing noise to break the quietness. It was only when it ran slowly over the cattlegrid that Pandora heard it and looked up. No wonder she hadn't heard it before; the car was a gleaming silver-grey Rolls-Royce, its engine running almost silently as it whispered its way over the bridge and pulled up at the foot of the double staircase leading to the entrance. James Arbory got out of the back of the car and then it pulled away again, the chauffeur driving it round to the garage block at the far side of the house.

Pandora stayed where she was, waiting for Sir James to go inside so that she could run back to the house herself, but instead of going in immediately, he looked around and paused to light a cigarette, then put his hands in his pockets as he, too, strolled down towards the lake. Shrinking back into the shadow of the tree, Pandora tried to make herself as small as possible, feeling an overwhelming reluctance to reveal her presence. He strolled down to within only about twenty feet of her, then stopped to lean his elbows on an ornate stonework pillar, one of a pair that stood at the top of some steps leading down to the lake. He leant there comfortably, smoking his cigarette, as if he did it often, and Pandora only then remembered her uncle's warning that Sir James often took a late night walk.

She wondered what he was thinking as he gazed out across the moonlit landscape, every bit of which belonged to him, every stick and stone as far as his eyes could see. Was he revelling in his suzerainty, feeding his arrogant pride with this silent survey of his estate, or was he—she smiled to herself—merely deciding that the grass needed cutting or the lake clearing? Somehow she had never associated such mundane matters with the nobility before.

James Arbory threw down the stub of his cigarette and straightened up. He was wearing a black evening suit that made him seem taller and broader somehow. But perhaps it was just a trick of the moonlight, the same moonlight that darkened the planes of his face giving him a lean, predatory look that was both dangerous and menacing.

No, she had no need to revise her opinion of her master, he was as hard and proud as she had first supposed, fully in control of his environment and ruthless in his determination to keep things that way. A man to be afraid of, not to try to fool with silly games.

He turned and looked straight towards where she sat huddled against the tree for a long moment, almost as if he could see her clearly, which she knew was impossible, but even so she shrank deeper into the darkness. Then he turned abruptly on his heel and strode purposefully back towards the house.

CHAPTER THREE

PANDORA managed to get through the next day without incurring her uncle's wrath and without seeing James Arbory, both because it was Sunday and their employer had gone out for the day, leaving early in the morning, so Uncle Charlie relaxed in a chair with the Sunday paper and magnanimously told her that she could have the rest of the day off after she had done all her chores. It was obvious that he wasn't going to stir an inch to help her, regarding this as a rest day, but Pandora merely laughed, rumpled what little hair he had left on his head so that he bellowed with annoyance and then ran upstairs willingly enough to tidy her employer's bedroom.

Her uncle had shown her what had to be done the day before, but somehow it still seemed strange to walk into someone else's room, to handle their things and see the way they lived. Not that you could tell much of James Arbory's character from his room, really; it was too neat for that, with very few things left lying around to give any clues. Just a pair of jade cufflinks on the dresser which she carefully put away in a drawer, a concert programme thrown into the wastepaper basket. Pandora squinted at it sidesays: so James Arbory liked Mozart, did he? Interesting. But apart from that she learnt little about her employer; the furniture, though mostly antique, wasn't overwhelmingly so. The bed, for instance, was a wide, comfortable half-tester and not the huge four-poster with heavy drapes that she had expected, so it wasn't too difficult to make with the clean linen that he insisted on every day—a luxury that made Pandora green with envy. The bathroom, though, was ultra-modern and super-luxurious, with a sunken bath big enough for about three people and containing one of those whirlpool devices that made the water bubble up and froth around you as you sat in it. Pandora was strongly tempted to try it out now that Sir James was safely out of the way, but thought of her uncle's face if he ever found out and contented herself with merely cleaning out the room.

With the rest of the day to herself, Pandora decided to explore the grounds and to go in the direction of the paddocks where she had seen the horses on her first day. From conversation with Uncle Charlie, she had learnt that Abbot's Arbory was fast getting a reputation for itself as a stud farm, a side of the estate that James Arbory had built up since coming into his inheritance five years ago. The weather was dry, but there was quite a strong breeze, so she plaited her hair into one long, thick braid down her back, pushed her feet into a pair of serviceable wellington boots, and put on a tweed jacket over her sweater.

The wind struck cold at first; Pandora turned up her collar and began to stride out towards the stables, but from behind her came the sound of barking and she turned to see the two dogs that had been with James Arbory on the day that he had thrown her off his land. She stood still immediately. Their master might not have recognised her without her leather gear, but the dogs certainly would, *and* they would remember her as someone to whom he had been antagonistic.

They stopped a few yards away, eyeing her warily and growling deep in their throats. They were beautiful dogs and in excellent condition; pointers, working dogs that James Arbory would take on shooting parties with him, and presumably they lived in one of the out-houses, because Pandora hadn't seen them in the house anywhere. She stayed very still and began to talk to them gently, using a soft lilting tone that her father had taught her when she was only a small child. Slowly the dogs' growls died away, their stances became less threatening and their ears came up. Pandora carefully extended a hand towards them and first one and then the other came to sniff at it. She didn't try to hurry them, let them take their time in making up their minds about her, still talking all the time in little more than a soft whisper. At last they began to lick her hand, their smooth long tails wagging in friendship. Then Pandora went down on to her knees to stroke and praise them.

'Good boy. Good dogs.' Still petting them, she searched along their collars for their name tags. 'So you're Thor and you're Odin. Very warlike names for such old softies!' She continued to make a fuss of them for a while, then stood up. The dogs immediately came to her heels, looking up at her expectantly. She laughed. 'Okay, you can come along, but don't blame me if your master finds out and gets mad.'

She set off again on her interrupted walk, playing with the dogs as she went, throwing them sticks and making them leap up to take things from her hand, all three of them enjoying themselves immensely, but at the entrance to the stableyard, which was nearly half a mile from the house, she hesitated, wondering if the dogs were allowed in. 'Sit,' she told them. 'Stay!' And they immediately obeyed, settling themselves down to wait for her.

Pandora went through the arched entranceway

topped by a bell tower, and found that the stableyard was a big hollow square with looseboxes all the way round. Most of the boxes had the upper halves of the doors open and several horses were looking out, but all the human activity seemed to be centred in one corner where three men were clustered round the open door of a box with number twelve over it. Curiosity being just one of her besetting sins, Pandora walked over to see what was going on.

The men were so intent on their conversation that they didn't notice her crossing the yard and she had time to observe them. The eldest of them was about fifty, dressed in a worn but serviceable tweed jacket and riding breeches. His face was tanned and leathery as if he worked in the open air all the time and he spoke with a marked country accent. The features of the man who stood next to him bore a striking resemblance, although the man was much younger, and Pandora guessed that they must be close relatives, probably father and son, but the younger man wore jeans and a thick sweater. The third man she instinctively put in a different class, possibly because his clothes, although just as practical, were better cut, or perhaps it was only because the other two men seemed to defer to him, to listen attentively when he spoke. He was about thirty, tall and fair-haired.

They were discussing a mare that was in foal and all three of them seemed to be anxious about it. Pandora came quietly up behind them and looked over their shoulders into the box. The horse inside was a magnificent Arab mare, a grey, with long mane and tail. She shone with health and good grooming, her head held elegantly high, tossing her mane arrogantly at being disturbed.

'Oh, she's beautiful!'

At Pandora's exclamation they all three turned round to stare at her in surprise. The youngest man gave an appreciative whistle as he looked her over, but it was the elder who said suspiciously, 'And who might you be, miss?'

For a moment she was in a quandary, wondering what to say, then thought she had better stick to the diminution of her name that her uncle had saddled her with. 'I'm Dora Smith. I'm the new maid.'

This admission immediately settled her place in the hierarchy and the older man said brusquely, 'Then you shouldn't be here. Your place is up at the house. Unless Sir James sent you?'

'No, he didn't send me. I just wanted to see the horses.'

'Then be off with you. This is a stud, not a riding stable. We don't allow people to stroll around whenever they feel like it.'

Both of the younger men came to her rescue, talking at once.

'She isn't doing any harm, Dad.'

'I'm quite sure Sir James wouldn't object.'

And the third man won as as he went on firmly, drowning out the other, 'One visitor hardly represents a flood, Mr Langley, and I'm sure it can do no harm to let her look round. He smiled at Pandora. 'I'm Jonathan Thursby, the local vet. And this is Mr Langley, the stud manager, and his son Tom.'

Pandora smiled at them all, her green eyes warm and friendly. 'How do you do. I'm sorry if I interrupted you when you were busy.' She turned the full brilliance of her eyes on Mr Langley, who seemed to be the only one in opposition. 'I didn't mean to intrude. The horses looked so lovely in the field, I just wanted to see them closer to.'

'Well . . .' He hesitated.

'Go on, Dad,' his son urged. 'I'll take her round and see she doesn't do any harm.'

'Or I've got half an hour to spare if you need Tom for something,' Jonathan Thursby put in smoothly, receiving a stabbing look from Tom for the suggestion.

'Well . . .' Mr Langley demurred again, then looked into Pandora's face, her eyes wide and wistful. 'Oh, all right, as it's Sunday and we're not very busy at the moment. But it's only for just this once, mind,' he added, wagging his finger at her.

'Oh, *thank* you, Mr Langley. You are kind. Where shall we start?'

In the end they all three took her round; Mr Langley enjoying showing off his charges as much as the others enjoyed escorting her. Several of the horses were mares brought to be covered by the Arab stallions at stud, but there were also some younger horses coming along and some mares that were owned by the stud itself. They ended up back at the box where the grey mare was in foal.

'What's her name?' Pandora asked as she admiringly stroked the mare's nose.

'Greymist,' Jonathan Thursby told her. 'We're taking extra special care of her. She's a very important lady. Sir James bought her in to improve the blood line and this will be her first foal, so we're all hoping it will be successful.'

'Is there any danger?'

'Not really.' He too came to stroke the mare's neck. 'But mares are always nervous the first time. Especially sensitive beauties like this.'

The tour ended, Pandora thanked Mr Langley and his son warmly and turned to leave, but the older man surprised her by saying rather gruffly, 'As you're here, lass, you might as well come over to the house and meet Tom's mother. I expect she'll have a cup of tea on the go.'

Tom's face broke into a big grin and Jonathan Thursby's eyebrows rose at the suggestion. 'You're honoured, Dora. Not many people get invited to Mr Langley's on such a short acquaintance.'

Pandora smiled warmly. 'I know I am, and I'd love to accept, but the dogs followed me here and I've left them sitting by the gate all this time and I just can't leave them any longer, poor things.'

Tom Langley frowned. 'Dogs? You don't mean Sir James' pointers?'

'Yes, that's right. Thor and Odin.'

They all looked at her in astonishment.

'Well, I'll be——' Mr Langley exclaimed. 'I've never known those dogs to take to anyone but Sir James.' He chuckled. 'The last maid they had up at the house was scared to death of them. But don't worry about bringing them, I expect the wife can find them a titbit or two.'

Whether the invitation had included him or not wasn't quite clear, but Jonathan Thursby tagged along all the same, blandly ignoring Tom's offer not to keep him if he was busy. Mrs Langley was a buxom, friendly woman who had herself once been a parlourmaid at the big house, and Pandora spent a very pleasant hour drinking first tea and then Mrs Langley's home-made gooseberry wine and eating freshly baked scones, still hot from the oven and dripping with butter and strawberry jam.

She learnt a lot about Abbot's Arbory in that hour

and quite a bit about Sir James, as Mrs Langley had known him since he was born.

'The estate had run down quite a bit before he inherited,' the older woman confided. 'That was because his father, Sir Edward, that was, had been ill for a long time, but not so bad that he'd hand over completely to his son, as he should have done. But Sir James has done wonders since he took over—built up the farm and repaired all the houses on the estate and in the village that he owns, as well as turning the stables into a stud. Worked all hours of the day, he did, when he first took over, what with putting the estate and the house to rights as well as seeing to all his business interests in London. Did very well, he did, in business, by all accounts. He put all his energy into that, you see, when his father was alive and when he wasn't allowed to help with the estate.'

This began to sound intriguing, but unfortunately Mr Langley overheard and told his wife off for letting her tongue run away with her. Pandora took this as a hint and stood up to go.

'I really must be getting back to the house now or Mr Richardson will think I've got lost or something. Thank you so much, I've enjoyed myself immensely.'

Mrs Langley escorted her to the door. 'You must come again some time.' She didn't exactly say it, but the expressive look on her face said clearly, some time when the men aren't here and we can have a good gossip.

Jonathan Thursby took his leave at the same time and walked along beside her, Thor and Odin at her heels.

'Do you know this part of the country at all?' he asked her.

Pandora shook her head. 'No, I've never been here before.'

'In that case perhaps you'd like to come on my rounds with me one day. I get to cover quite a large area on my different calls, and as you're so good with animals it would probably interest you to see something of my work.'

'That's very kind of you, Mr Thursby,' Pandora began, 'but . . .'

'The name's Jon,' he broke in with a grin. 'When you call me Mr Thursby it makes you sound like a customer who owes me money.'

Pandora laughed. 'Okay—Jon.' She smiled at him, liking his typically English good looks and the open friendliness of his manner. 'I'd like to go with you, but as yet I'm a very new maid, in fact I only started properly yesterday, so it might be difficult to arrange.'

'You must get a day off at least.'

'Yes, but I haven't really got round to discussing it with the butler yet. I might have to fit it round whether Sir James is entertaining guests or not. I'm not really sure; I haven't had a job like this before,' she confessed.

'Well, Sir James will make sure you get your share of time off. He's always very fair with his staff. If you like I'll ask him to let you have a day off during the week.'

'Oh, no,' Pandora said hastily. 'I'd much rather work it out with the butler.' He nodded and after a moment she said, 'Do you know him that well, then? Sir James, I mean.'

'Quite well. Mainly through my job, of course. But we're both members of the cricket club and on the board of the local P.D.S.A., that sort of thing.'

They reached his car and he offered to give her a lift back to the house, but Pandora steadfastly refused, merely shaking hands as she said goodbye and then turning to walk back towards the house, the dogs ranging along beside her.

Monday was a busy day, starting with the arrival early in the morning of the three dailies who were all women from the village. They were nice enough, but privately Pandora christened them the three witches, because every time they came together they gossiped inexhaustibly in their broad dialect so that there always seemed to be a babble of noise rising and falling wherever they went. What they thought of Pandora she didn't know, because as soon as they heard that she was from London they treated her as a foreigner, as unlike themselves as someone from Peking or Timbuctoo.

Luckily her duties didn't overlap with theirs too much and she was able to go about her tasks without getting in their way, although Uncle Charlie twice had to tell her off for whistling as she worked. 'Young ladies don't whistle,' he reproved her. 'And Sir James certainly wouldn't like it if he heard it. Here, take this clean laundry up to that big linen cupboard near Sir James' room. And walk up the stairs, don't run up them two at a time!' he admonished her.

'Okay, Uncle Charlie, will do.' She gave him a mock salute and marched out of the kitchen with the pile of linen in her arms as if she was on parade. Her uncle gave a groaning sigh and raised his eyes heavenwards.

Pandora reached the linen cupboard without whistling, running, or dropping the sheets, which she thought was pretty good, considering, and carefully laid the bed linen and towels out on the old oak shelves that smelt of the lavender of a hundred summers. Closing the door, she turned to go back to the kitchen, but noticed that the door of a bedroom further down the corridor was ajar. Thinking that one of the cleaners had left it open, she went to shut it, but couldn't resist looking inside first as this wasn't one of the rooms that her uncle had shown her over. She took one glance at the four-poster bed inside and went in for a closer look.

It was a very feminine room; the hangings on the four-poster were in soft creamy lace and the walls painted a pale pink with a deep-piled carpet in a darker matching tone. A three-mirrored dressing table stood near the windows and there was another, full-length mirror over in the corner. Definitely a woman's room! She crossed over to the big wardrobe and opened it. There were some clothes inside and her eyebrows rose as she went through them: a fashionable tweed jacket and matching skirt, a sophisticated evening dress, a bathrobe, a pair of riding breeches, and, last of all, a slinky black nightdress that couldn't have left a lot to the imagination. All good clothes and in a size not much larger than Pandora's own. In the bottom of the wardrobe there was also a pair of riding boots, and a pair of high-heeled fluffy mules, again in black to match the nightdress, presumably. Pandora stood back to contemplate these for a moment, then pulled out the drawers of the dresser where there were a couple of sweaters and some delicate lacy underwear, the sort that look made out of nothing but cost a fortune. Pandora thought of her own much laundered undies and shut the drawer firmly. On the dressing table there was a bottle of French perfume and some make-up, and she found a few other feminine cosmetics, bath oil and that kind of thing, in the adjoining bathroom.

It seemed that Sir James had a guest, someone fairly young and fashionable, going by the clothes, who came to stay frequently but only for short visits, often enough to lay claim to the room but not long enough to leave any more permanent belongings other than clothes. No photographs or books, for example. Intriguing.

Pandora took a last look round the room, trying to guess who the woman could be and what she would look like.

Back in the kitchen she found Uncle Charlie fussing around trying to do three jobs at once.

'Sir James has just phoned to say that he's bringing two guests to lunch. He said anything would do, but I know he'll expect at least a four-course meal. Where's that gardener with the vegetables? I told him I wanted them right away. Oh, and there's the wine still to be brought up from the cellars. And you'll have to set the table, Pandora.'

Pandora looked at him in some amusement, then took pity on him and firmly took the basin he was holding out of his hands. 'Uncle, why don't *I* cook the lunch while you see to the wine and the table? What were you going to use all these eggs for—omelettes? I thought so.' She gently shooed him out of her way and he went willingly enough, raising only a half-hearted protest.

Left to herself, Pandora happily set about preparing the meal—but without the omelettes. She much enjoyed cooking and had taken several specialised courses in the past, mainly so that she could get a job as a chalet hostess in Switzerland during the winter holidays, which she had done for the last two years. When she was about fourteen she had even contemplated taking up cookery as a career, but she had too much intelligence and curiosity to want to be tied to a kitchen all her working life and she had decided instead to go on to university.

The gardener, an elderly man and inclined to be surly, eventually turned up with the vegetables, but after Pandora had sat him down, given him a bottle of beer and got him talking about his beloved gardens, he mellowed quite a bit and confided that 'that there townie butler' didn't know a thing about the difficulties a gardener faced and kept expecting him to supply out-of-season fruit and vegetables 'as if I were a magician with a wand and a top 'at.'

Pandora sympathised with him, gave him another beer and suggested he bring what vegetables he had up to the house every morning and she would adapt her menus accordingly. When he left he called her 'a right good lass' and she rather thought she had made a friend for life.

Uncle Charlie served Sir James and his guests with home-made mushroom soup, grilled trout with almonds, and chicken in wine sauce followed by a strawberry flan and cream. Nothing really elaborate because Pandora hadn't had the time, but when her uncle came down into the kitchen at the end of the meal he graciously informed her that her new employer had sent his compliments. Spoiling the effect rather by adding, 'So you might as well take over the cooking while you're here. At least you don't seem accident-prone in the kitchen.' And Pandora realised she had lumbered herself with another job.

While they were eating their own lunch she said casually, 'Has Sir James got any sisters?'

'Sisters? No, he's an only child.'

'No female relatives at all?' Pandora persisted.

'Only an aunt who comes over to act as hostess whenever he has a hunt ball or a really big house-party. I expect she'll be coming over next month for the Rose Ball.'

Pandora was instantly diverted. 'The Rose Ball—what's that?'

'It's a tradition here,' her uncle explained. 'A ball is

held every year when the roses are in bloom. It goes back to when Charles II was restored to the throne and he came here to thank the contemporary owner of Abbot's Arbory for supporting him in the war against Cromwell's Roundheads. A ball was given for him then and has been held ever since.'

The idea was enchanting and Pandora let her imagination run riot for several minutes as she pictured the original ball with the Merry Monarch and his court here in their gorgeous costumes, dancing in the rooms and gardens, lit by candles and moonlight, the women vying for the King's attention. But this thought brought her mind back to the present and she asked, 'This aunt—how old is she?'

'Lady Townley? Oh, she must be about sixty, I should think. Why?'

'Oh, nothing really,' Pandora answered, trying to sound casual. 'It's just that I saw some women's clothes in one of the bedrooms and I wondered if Sir James had a relative who came to stay.'

'Hmph—those!' Her uncle sniffed rather disdainfully. 'Those belong to Miss Marsden.'

'Who's she?'

'Just a friend of Sir James',' he replied repressively.

'What kind of friend?'

'She has an antique shop in Oxford and Sir James buys pieces from her now and again.'

'You'd think he had enough of them already,' Pandora remarked, remembering the amount of dusting she had to do. 'Is she a close friend?'

'Who?'

'This Miss Marsden you're telling me about.'

'I'm not telling you about her,' her uncle retorted in some annoyance. 'It's you who keeps asking about her.'

He tried to change the subject. 'Pour me out another cup of coffee, would you? And then you can put the rest of the dirty crockery in the dishwasher.'

But Pandora poured out two cups of coffee instead of one and sat down opposite him again. 'Well, how close a friend is she?'

He stirred his coffee resignedly. 'I believe they've known each other for years.'

'That doesn't tell me how close they are. I've known several people for years and we're not close friends.'

'That hardly surprises me,' her uncle replied at his most repressive.

Pandora chuckled. 'Come on, Uncle Charlie, spill the beans! Is this Miss Marsden Sir James' mistress?'

He choked on his coffee so that Pandora had to leap up and bang him on the back.

'All right! I'm all right.' He looked at her indignantly. 'Really! The young these days have absolutely no sense of decorum. Why, in my day . . .' He broke off when he saw the look on her face. 'Fancy asking me a question like that! How would I know? I don't go around prying into Sir James' personal life.'

'Oh, come on,' Pandora said persuasively. 'Servants always know everything there is to know about their employers.'

Exasperatedly her uncle said, 'Well, even if I did I certainly wouldn't discuss such a subject with you, young lady, because it's definitely none of your business.'

'Which means that she is his mistress,' said Pandora with some satisfaction. 'What's her first name?'

Automatically he answered, 'Cynthia.' Then in real anger, he added forcefully, 'And now I forbid you to say another word about it. Do you hear me, Pandora? You are not to mention the matter again.'

Having got all the information she wanted out of him, Pandora took the wind out of his sails by saying meekly, 'Very well, Uncle. I won't tell anyone you told me,' and gurgled with suppressed laughter at the expression of surprise and consternation on his face.

But it was Pandora's turn for consternation later that day when her uncle came down into the kitchen after serving dinner and said, 'Sir James has said that you can go into Oxford tomorrow and get yourself a new uniform. You're to meet him in the front hall promptly at nine-thirty.'

Pandora looked at him in surprise. 'What do you mean—meet him in the front hall?'

'Sir James has to go into Oxford himself tomorrow to attend a meeting and he says you can drive in with him.'

'But I don't want to drive there with him, I'd rather go on my motorbike,' Pandora wailed.

'Well, you can hardly tell him that, can you?'

'No, I suppose not.' Pandora looked at him dejectedly. 'And I was looking forward to going to Oxford, too. I've never been there before.'

'Well, you won't have to spend the whole day with him. Only the hour's drive there and back,' Uncle Charlie pointed out reasonably.

But the thought of even two hours in Sir James' company somehow filled her with foreboding and took all the pleasure and anticipation out of the trip. It also kept her awake part of the night, her biggest fear being that during two hours her phoney accent might slip and he would find her out, but by the next morning she had hit upon a way round the difficulty and was waiting for him in the hall on the dot of nine-thirty, dressed in one of her own jumpers and skirts and a navy blue mac left over from her schooldays.

Sir James, too, was prompt. He was wearing a dark business suit and carrying a briefcase, which somehow made him seem more intimidating than in his country tweeds. Perhaps it was because it gave a cleaner line to the hardness of his jaw, sharpened his already lean features. His grey eyes under the slightly arched brows ran over her as she stood beside her uncle.

'Good morning, Dora.'

She didn't answer but fell in behind him as Uncle Charlie opened the door and he went down the steps to the waiting Rolls.

He nodded to the chauffeur who was holding the back door open for him. 'It's all right, Travers, I'll drive myself today.'

'Very good, sir.' The chauffeur sprang to open the driver's door instead and Pandora took the opportunity to dive like a squirrel into the back seat. Sir James looked round for her, his eyebrows rising slightly as he saw that she was already in, but he made no comment, merely starting the softly purring engine and setting off down the drive.

Pandora looked back at the house as they drove away, loving this view of the mansion set among its parkland with the sun glistening on the lake; watched until the trees hid it from view. The Lodge gates were already open, a boy standing by them, and they swept through and turned to the right, away from the village and in a direction Pandora hadn't travelled before. Ordinarily she would have been looking through the windows at the perfect Cotswold scenery of long, undulating hills and picturesque villages, but she had never been in a Rolls-Royce before and was busily taking in all the luxurious fittings. The upholstery was in the softest leather, the seats deep and comfortable and there was a console built into the armrest near her hand with several buttons to operate all the electronic gadgets in the car. Pandora peered at them: windows, air-conditioning, heater, radio, television, bar, telephone. Her eyebrows rose at the last three and she would dearly have loved to press the buttons, but didn't dare. Her fingers stroked the smooth upholstery; impossible not to be impressed with such luxury, but then she thought how much it had cost and how many tractors could be bought for poor farmers in third world countries for that money to help them produce food for the starving, and she was filled with an impotent stab of rage. How *could* one man have so much when hundreds of thousands had nothing at all? She gazed out of the window at the fields rich with crops, the houses with gardens full of vegetables and fruit trees, the shops bursting with goods, and her heart filled with bewilderment and anger at the apparent inability of the world's leaders to set the balance right.

She was so consumed by her own thoughts that she didn't notice that Sir James had pulled in to the side of the road and had stopped the car. He turned towards her, his arm along the back of the seat, a slight smile on his lips, but his expression changed when he saw the unhappiness on her face and he frowned.

'Is something the matter, Dora?'

The sound of his voice made her jump and brought her rudely back to the present. She stared at him for a moment and then shook her head.

'Then come and sit in the front with me.' It wasn't a suggestion but a definite order.

She shook her head again. 'Mr Richardson said as how I was to sit in the back,' she replied hoarsely.

'But I'm telling you to come and sit in the front.'

For a moment longer she gazed at him, wondering how she could get out of it, then reluctantly opened the door and walked round to sit beside him, carefully not looking at him directly.

He looked at her quizzically for a moment, then leant towards her.

Pandora immediately flinched away, but he merely said, 'I'm only going to do your safety strap up for you,' and reached past her to pull the strap down and clip it into place. Then he drew back, but continued to look at her. 'You're not afraid of me, are you, Dora?'

Her eyes flew to his face, to see the slight look of amusement still there, then quickly away again. She shook her head dumbly.

'Good. You certainly weren't before.'

He waited for a moment, but when she didn't answer, her face still averted, he frowned slightly, then turned away to start the car again. 'I hear you went over to the stables on Sunday,' he remarked.

Now who told him *that*? Pandora wondered, but he went on, 'Do you like horses?'

When she didn't answer straightaway he glanced towards her and she nodded assent.

'Then maybe I'll arrange for you to have riding lessons. Would you like that?'

Riding lessons—for a maid? Who did he think he was kidding? Firmly she shook her head.

He frowned, then brought the car to a stop again. 'What's the matter, Dora, cat got your tongue? You're not usually so reticent.'

'I got a sore throat,' she lied hoarsely.

He was immediately all concern. 'Richardson should have told me. But how lucky that we're on our way to Oxford; my doctor has a practice there and we can easily go there first so that he can take a look at you.'

A look of alarm came into Pandora's eyes and she chokily muttered something about 'throat lozenges' and 'be all right.'

But James Arbory said firmly, 'No, I must insist that you see a doctor. Sore throats can often be the first sign of something far worse. Pneumonia, for instance,' he added mendaciously.

Pandora looked at him balefully, hating him. 'It ain't as bad as that,' she was forced to admit in something approaching her normal voice.

'Good, then you'll be able to talk to me, won't you? Now, you like horses but you don't want to learn to ride, is that right?'

'Yes, Sir James,' she agreed woodenly; no point in telling him that her father, who had been a pilot officer in the R.A.F. before his early death in a plane crash, had taught her to ride almost as soon as she could walk.

'You just like to look at them, is that it?'

'Yes, Sir James,' she agreed, her face expressionless.

An exasperated look came into his eyes. 'Dora, I shall become extremely angry with you in a minute. Why are you being so formal?'

Reluctantly she turned to look at him. Still in her broad Cockney accent she answered, 'Mr Richardson told me off. 'E said I was always to call you Sir James and only speak when I was spoken to.'

'Did he, indeed? And did he also say that you were only to answer yes or no?'

Pandora decided to blame her poor uncle even further. ' 'E told me to keep me mouth shut as much as I could, 'cos I don't talk proper.'

To her surprise, instead of laughing his face softened. 'So you pretended to have a sore throat so that you wouldn't have to speak to me?' He hesitated, then, 'Are you ashamed of the way you speak, Dora? Because if so

I might be able to do something to help you. Elocution lessons, for example.'

So now he saw himself as Professor Higgins to her Eliza Doolittle, did he? Well, she would squash that idea on the head straightaway. 'No,' she retorted defiantly, 'why should I be ashamed? Just because I don't talk posh like you. I talk the same as all me mates in London, and if you don't like it you can always gimme the sack. They didn't tell me at the agency that I 'ad to speak wiv a plum in me mouth for this job.'

'No more you do.' James Arbory looked at her steadily for a moment, then smiled suddenly. 'And I much prefer your Cockney naturalness to that po-faced formality you tried earlier.'

Which statement so surprised her that she could only stare at him as he sat back with a chuckle and started the car again.

For the rest of the journey he talked to her about Oxford, it turning out that he had been to university there and knew the town well, and she managed to keep up her pretence of ignorance, resisting his attempts to draw her into conversation, although it was sometimes difficult to remember as she longed to ask him about the Bodleian Library and the history of the colleges, when all he told her about was the shops and trivialities about the town. But then she supposed he was talking down to her because he thought that was her level of intelligence—as if not speaking the same way as he did meant that you also lacked a brain! A thought that made Pandora's blood boil so that she was heartily glad when he pulled into a car park at the side of a large hotel.

He took a card from his wallet. 'The shop you want is just off the High Street. Here, I'll write the name and address on the back of my card.' He handed it to her. 'Show them this and tell them to charge the things to my account. Then come back and meet me here at one o'clock.' With a slight smile he added, 'Think you can remember all that?'

Pandora looked at him bleakly: even a complete fool could remember that! But she merely said coldly, 'Yes, Sir James.'

His eyes flicked up to her face and his voice hardened. 'Good. Then don't be late. I dislike being kept waiting.'

Pandora hurried along to the shop, one which specialised in 'domestic attire' as they termed it and had models in the windows wearing a chef's outfit and a chauffeur's uniform. Production of Sir James' card assured her of immediate service, but she took no pleasure in trying on the new uniform and surprised the assistants by the speed in which she made up her mind and completed her purchases. Within half an hour she was out of the shop and into the sunshine, eager to make the most of the little time she had left to explore the town.

For a couple of hours she wandered happily round the streets and the parts of the colleges that were open to the public, but a glance at her watch told her that it was almost one already and she turned regretfully to make her way back to the car park, promising herself a much longer visit on her next day off.

James Arbory was waiting for her at the entrance to the car park, but to her surprise he led her not back to the car, but to the entrance to the hotel.

Seeing her puzzled look, he said, 'I thought we might have lunch here. You can leave your parcel with your coat in the cloakroom.'

Pandora looked round the marble-pillared foyer, busy with richly-dressed people, and through the door to the restaurant, all hurrying waiters, snowy-white cloths and deep plush carpet. Then she remembered her own shabby skirt and sweater and for a moment her heart failed her. She opened her mouth to say, 'But I can't . . .' then looked into her employer's face and the words died away. He was regarding her steadily, his left eyebrow slightly raised and a distinct challenge in his eyes. Pandora's chin came up defiantly, mentally picking up his gauntlet. So he thought she was afraid, did he? Well, she'd show him that she was as good as all those toffee-nosed snobs any day! And maybe she'd make him sorry into the bargain. So she said quite loudly, 'I'll go and 'ang me coat up, then.'

But for all her bravado, in the cloakroom Pandora took care to comb her hair into some sort of order and apply her lipstick carefully. She looked ruefully at the skirt and jumper, and sighed—if she'd only known that he was going to take her out to lunch. Then she shrugged; not that it would have made any difference if he had told her, she still wouldn't have had any suitable clothes to wear. She just wasn't in the habit of being taken out to lunch in posh restaurants by wealthy baronets. Lifting her head, she regarded her reflection in the mirror thoughtfully, wondering if the rich baronet in question was in the habit of taking his maids out to lunch. Somehow she rather thought not. 'Which means, my girl,' she told her mirrored image, 'that you'd better watch it. The man is obviously trying to turn your head so that he can achieve his evil intentions.' And she leered at herself in the glass, so that the woman in the fur jacket standing next to her stared at her in astonishment, then hurriedly picked up her belongings and

almost ran out of the cloakroom, which made Pandora
double up with laughter.

It seemed that Sir James was well known at the hotel,
for the head waiter greeted him by name and himself
led them to a discreetly placed table in an alcove with a
big window overlooking the river. An underling placed
a menu in her hands and her eyebrows rose at the exotic
choice of dishes, none of which had the prices by them,
she noticed. Did that make the clientele so rich that
they didn't care how much they paid? Why, you could
probably feed a whole African or Indian village for the
cost of one meal here!

Her indignant thoughts were interrupted as Sir James
said smoothly, 'Perhaps you'd like me to choose for
you, Dora. The veal here is excellent.'

Veal! Trust these bloated plutocrats to eat the flesh of
poor, newly-born calves! Her eyes sparking, she said
distinctly, 'No, thank you. I would like soup followed by
a salad.'

His eyes came up quickly to her face, an arrested
look in them, and she realised that she had forgotten
her phoney accent. Quickly she tried to retrieve the slip
by adding, 'I ain't very 'ungry.'

He nodded and turned to the waiter to give the order,
waving away the wine list as he asked for a certain vin-
tage with which he was obviously familiar.

Turning to face her, Sir James sat back in his chair,
his dark eyes watching her contemplatively. 'You know,
Dora,' he said slowly, 'you're rather an enigma.'

She returned his look warily. So he wanted to play
verbal games, did he? Well, she could serve a few aces
herself. Opening her eyes wide, she replied, 'Oh, no, I
ain't. I'm a Londoner. I was born in 'Ackney.'

A quick gleam of laughter came into his eyes but was

immediately suppressed as he said gravely, 'I'm sure that Hackney was a very good place to be born in, but that wasn't quite what I meant. An enigma means something or someone that is mysterious and puzzling, has hidden depths.'

Pandora picked up her fork and made patterns with it on the crisp whiteness of the tablecloth. 'And why do you think I'm one of these enigma things? There's nothin' mysterious about me.'

'Isn't there? I rather think there is.'

She looked at him uneasily, not liking the turn the conversation had taken. Had he seen through her already?

Without waiting for her to answer, James Arbory went on, 'This is the twentieth century, Dora. Girls who look like you don't usually become domestic servants. They try to get into modelling or acting, often via beauty contests. And if they don't succeed there or don't have that much ambition, they at least try for a more interesting or glamorous job—such as an air stewardess or something similar. Haven't you ever tried for something like that? Or ever wanted to?'

Pandora returned his look angrily. What a typical male chauvinist attitude! Just because a girl had a decent face and figure men thought she ought to be in a job where looks were all that mattered. It never occurred to them that there might be a brain behind a pretty face and that a girl might want more out of her work than just showing herself off until she got too old and crabby to be employable. And personally she would hate such a career; the everlasting fight to keep yourself looking young, the backbiting and spitefulness of other girls fighting for the few jobs there were, having to look glamorous all the time and to be pleasant and smiling even when you felt like death. No, thank you very much, that kind of life certainly wasn't for her. She wanted something with a challenge, where she could use her intelligence and work on her own initiative, to have a career that would last her through life and she could always fall back on, no matter what.

Shortly she answered, 'No. I'm all right as I am,' and glared at him rather defiantly.

His eyes held hers for a long moment, then he said abruptly, 'How old are you, Dora?'

'I'm twenty,' she returned automatically, but had little time to wonder why he had asked because the waiter came up with their first course, making a welcome interruption.

She concentrated on eating her soup, feeling uneasy and wishing that the meal would soon be over, but Sir James took his time over his avocado stuffed with prawns and insisted that she try the glass of wine that the waiter had poured out for her. Pandora sipped it gingerly at first but with growing appreciation; it was far superior to the supermarket plonk that was the usual drink her college friends managed to afford whenever there was some sort of event to be celebrated, usually birthdays or the passing of an exam.

While she waited for him to finish, Pandora looked around her at the other diners. There were only a few couples like themselves, mostly there were trios or quartets of women, gossiping about their shopping, or of men on what were obviously prolonged and expensive business lunches. And all on their expense accounts, Pandora thought cynically. She watched one man push his plate away, the large steak on it only half eaten, a woman try a mouthful of gateau, decide she didn't like it and call the waiter over to replace it with something else.

Turning to Sir James she said abruptly, 'What happens to all the waste?'

He looked startled. 'I beg your pardon?'

'The waste food,' Pandora said impatiently. 'What happens to it?'

His eyebrows rose. 'I have no idea.'

'No, I don't suppse you have,' Pandora retorted, much incensed. 'You rich people are all the same. You couldn't care less about the other half of the world. They can all starve to death for all you care! Just look at the food that's being wasted in this room. Why don't the people just take enough for what they want instead of being so greedy? And look at them—they're nearly all so fat that it would do them good to eat less. Heaven help them if they had to spend a week on what the people in the third world countries had to live on. Perhaps that would make them appreciate what they've got,' she added heatedly.

'I'm sure it would.' The words were said mildly enough, but it made Pandora glance at her host sharply. She found him watching her closely, the arrested look back in his eyes, an amused twist to the corner of his mouth. She flushed and looked away, taking a long drink of her wine, aware that her tongue had run away with her.

He leaned forward and filled her glass again. 'Are you a Communist, Dora?' he asked calmly.

'No, of course I'm not.' She looked away, playing with the stem of her glass.

'But you believe that the earth's products should be shared out more fairly?'

'Yes, I do.' Her head came up and she looked at him defiantly. 'And I believe that the land should be shared out too. I think it's wrong that only one per cent of the people should own ninety per cent of the country.'

'So you think that estates like Abbot's Arbory should be parcelled up and given away to people to use as allotments, do you?' James Arbory asked drily.

A waiter unobtrusively put the next course in front of them, but Pandora hardly noticed. 'Something along those lines, yes. Not necessarily allotments, of course—it would have to be worked out properly—but it's totally unfair that one person should have so much when others are crowded together in high-rise flats or grotty little houses without even a garden for the children to play in.'

'So you think the house should be pulled down and a housing estate built there, do you?'

That made Pandora pause. She thought for a minute and then shook her head. 'No, it's too beautiful for that. It ought to be preserved, but it ought to be shared. Why, you don't even open it to the public.'

His voice hardening, he said, 'Maybe that's because I believe that everyone has a certain right to privacy. Abbot's Arbory is my home. Would you like people tramping through your home? Going through your rooms and gaping at your most cherished possessions, things that have been treasured by your family and lovingly handed down from generation to generation?' His voice grew angry. 'Would you like to have massive car and coach parks where there was once a garden, public lavatories in the stables, ticket booths and souvenir stalls by the lodge gates and boat rides on the lake? Is that how you'd like to see Abbot's Arbory? Is it?'

Pandora stared at him, taken aback by his vehemence. It had never occurred to her to look at it from the owner's point of view before, and, having come to love the house, even though she had only been there for a few days, she could understand now what an anathema the idea must be to him who loved it so much more. Haltingly she said, 'I'm—I'm sorry. I hadn't thought of it like that before.'

'No. Not you or the countless others who want to nationalise the land, wrest it from those who've nurtured and cultivated it through the ages. The system of land ownership has evolved because it's right for the country and for farming. If it was parcelled up as you envisage we wouldn't produce half the crops and the country would go under in less than a decade.'

He took a long drink of his wine and looked at her consideringly, his eyes narrowed. 'And I suppose you also think that all people are equal?'

Pandora looked at him indignantly. 'Yes, of course I do.'

'Well, you're wrong, Dora, because they're not. It so happens that . . .'

But Pandora interrupted him before he could go on. 'Oh, I *know* that,' she said sarcastically. 'In a capitalist society there are always inequalities of class and wealth. People who inherit money and property will always see themselves as being superior to those who have to work for it.'

His mouth set into a thin line at her implied rudeness. 'There is also the basic inequality of being born either with a natural talent or without one. Clever or stupid. No matter how much you try to argue against it, Dora, we are not born equal. All man can ever strive for is the equality of opportunity for those who have the ability to make the most of it. There are always those who will succeed and those who have no ambition or ability who will fall by the wayside.'

'But you can't deny that those who have money have far more opportunity than those who haven't?'

'Not entirely, no. But I believe that a person with brain enough can go as high as he wishes.' He paused, then said more gently, 'What you want will come, Dora, but it will take time. And the last thing we want is a revolution to try and hurry it along.'

He regarded her steadily for a long moment, until Pandora looked away, feeling confused by his arguments; her ideas that had been so clearcut before now seemed childish and immature.

For a few minutes they ate in silence, then James Arbory said, 'Dora, if you believe that all people are equal, then presumably you think that no one should be subservient to another, right?'

Pandora looked at him cautiously, wondering where he was leading. 'Yes, basically,' she admitted.

He leaned forward, his eyes holding hers. 'In that case why did you choose to become my servant?'

CHAPTER FOUR

PANDORA stared at Sir James speechlessly for a long moment that seemed to go on for ever, completely trapped by his question. He watched her intently, his eyebrows raised quizzically as he waited for her answer.

'Well, I—I . . .' she floundered, unable to think of anything that would satisfy him, then gave a gasp of relief as the waiter came up to ask if they would like a dessert.

James Arbory sat back in his seat, a wry smile on his lips when he saw that she had escaped answering. 'Would you like anything else?'

She shook her head. 'No, thank you.'

He glanced at his watch. 'Then I think we might as well leave.'

He paid the bill while Pandora got her coat, and this time he made no objection when she determinedly got in the back seat, quite unable to face another argument with him. Or any kind of conversation, come to that. She had the uneasy conviction that he was the type of man you could never argue with, who would always shoot down your opinions in flames and leave you feeling like a first-form schoolgirl. So she sat alone in the back, still smarting and thinking over what he had said, and it wasn't until they had gone several miles that it suddenly occurred to her that in the heat of the argument she had completely forgotten her phoney accent and had spoken in her normal voice!

Now what was she going to do? Pandora stared malevolently at the back of his head, his dark, well-cut hair just touching his collar. Impossible to hope that he might not have noticed, so why hadn't he said something at the time? Because he was involved in their argument and didn't want to be sidetracked? Because he didn't think it worth mentioning? Or—and this she didn't like at all—because he had already seen through her and it came as no surprise? She stirred uneasily in her seat, angry with herself for having got carried away, and wondering if James Arbory would pick her up on it. No, not if, when. Because somehow she was quite sure that no way would he let her off scot free.

When they reached the house she muttered a hasty thank you and almost ran into the house clutching her parcel, scuttling past Uncle Charlie, who gave her a startled look as he hurried forward to open the car door for Sir James. Later he asked her how she had got on, but she merely told him that she had wandered round Oxford, feeling strangely reluctant to tell him that she had actually lunched with their employer. He had very definite ideas about the line drawn between master and servants and certainly wouldn't have approved, and it would only have raised added complications that Pandora could well do without.

For the next week or so she managed to avoid meeting Sir James, making sure that he was out of the way when she tidied the rooms he used and dodging back to the kitchen by the back stairs when he returned to the house. He was out to lunch most of the time, but she continued to cook his breakfast and evening meal which her uncle served as usual, but several times he passed on a message of appreciation for her cooking.

During the afternoons Uncle Charlie gave her a couple of hours off and she loved to explore the gardens, walking between the long banks of rhododendron bushes, their red, mauve and purple flowers a blaze of colour in the still summer air, or exploring the summerhouse on the edge of the lake and spending lazy hours on the seat there, the book on her lap neglected as she watched bright blue dragonflies darting over the lily-pads and waited, hardly daring to breathe, as a heron flew down and patiently looked for a fish to pluck from the water. But mostly she was drawn to the paddocks where she would sit on a fence and watch the horses as they frolicked in the fields, enthralled by their beauty and gracefulness, and to the stables where Mr Langley, to the surprise of everyone, let her help to groom one or two of the less valuable horses under his careful super-vision. She enjoyed this immensely and grew fond of all the horses, but her favourite was Greymist, for whom she always had some lumps of sugar purloined from the kitchen and who soon got to know her and would come to the stable door with a whicker of expectant welcome, nuzzling her hands as Pandora stroked her and nudging her until she got the sugar lumps.

'You'll spoil that horse,' Tom Langley told her, coming up to lean against the wall and watch. 'She's really taken to you, though. Usually she's nervous of people. Aren't you, lass?' He reached up to stroke her head, but the mare shied away and went back into the stable. 'There, you see. She doesn't want to know me.'

Pandora laughed. 'Maybe you don't speak to her properly. You have to tell horses how beautiful they are, you know. Flatter them until they eat out of your hand.'

'Is that the trick?' He looked at her, his eyes openly admiring her slim figure in blue denim dungarees, and said in a clumsy attempt at wit, 'I'll have to start flatter-ing you, then. I wouldn't mind having you eating out of my hand.'

'Oh, but I'm not a horse,' Pandora returned lightly. 'And I'd see through flattery straightaway.'

She went to turn aside, but Tom put his arm against the wall, barring her way. 'Flattery or not, you're still a good-looking bird. How about coming to the cinema with me tonight?'

'Thanks, but I have to cook dinner for Sir James,' she replied shortly, and turned the other way, intending to walk away from him.

But Tom swiftly put out his other arm so that she was trapped between them, leaning against the wall. 'So come down to the pub for a drink when you've finished, then. It doesn't take you all night to cook and clear up, does it?'

Pandora looked up at him in some annoyance; she supposed he was nice enough, but she didn't like the way he was trying to throw his weight around, putting on this he-man act in an attempt to either impress or coerce her. She opened her mouth to reject his suggestion, but as she did so he leaned forward to try to kiss her. Angrily she lifted her hands to his chest to try to push him away.

Then from behind Tom a crisp voice said, 'I believe I asked for a horse to be saddled for me at three o'clock,' and Pandora looked over Tom's shoulder to see James Arbory watching them with a disdainful frown on his face. Tom sprang away from her guiltily and Pandora flushed, realising how it must have looked to him.

'I'll get the horse for you now, sir.'

Tom rushed off towards the tack room and left her facing Sir James. For a moment their eyes met and held, then Pandora quickly turned away and hurried through the nearby arch leading out of the stables. As she did so she heard him call her name, but she pretended not to hear and kept on going, feeling completely unable to face him again.

She didn't stop until she got to the house where she

sought solace in the library, out of breath from hurrying and feeling strangely agitated. She sank down on a
comfortable red leather chesterfield and looked around
her at the room which had soon become her favourite
of the whole house. It was circular in shape and two
storeys high, with three long windows in the south-
facing wall so that sunlight streamed in all day long,
lighting the rows of bookshelves and the gallery above,
again lined with books. It was a room that didn't seem
to get used very much and Pandora often sneaked in
here for an hour or so after Uncle Charlie had gone to
bed, to gaze with awe at some of the titles and to handle
with reverent care one or two early editions of famous
works. She would dearly have loved to take a book to
her room to read, but was so overwhelmed by the rarity
of most of the works that she didn't dare in case they
should get marked, so she contented herself by just
looking at the rarer editions and reading those books
which were already well thumbed and which would be
difficult to find in an ordinary library, often becoming
so engrossed in a book that she stayed curled up in the
chesterfield until the early hours of the morning.

But right now she wasn't interested in reading, only
in the peaceful atmosphere of the room. Moodily she
wandered over to the window and looked out, angry
with herself for having got upset. What did it matter
what interpretation Sir James had put on that nasty
little scene with Tom, and why did she feel so guilty
even when she hadn't been doing anything? But
strangely enough it did matter; she hadn't liked that
cold, disdainful expression on his face when he had
looked at her, she had felt an overwhelming urge to
blurt out that it was none of her doing, that she had
been trying to push Tom away, not return his embrace.

But she hadn't, and she was glad. What the hell had it got to do with James Arbory if she wanted to flirt with Tom, or any other man, for that matter? He could frown as much as he liked, but it certainly wouldn't stop her from doing exactly as she liked in her free time. But then she remembered his anger and forcefulness when she had first met him, and she knew that she could never stand up to that sort of sheer animal menace again. A movement in the park caught her eyes and she looked up to see Sir James astride a big black stallion trotting away from the stables. He glanced towards the house and Pandora instinctively drew back, even though he could hardly have seen her from that distance, gripping the curtain, her hand going to her throat as if she found it difficult to breathe.

That evening her uncle brought her another message from Sir James. 'He wants to hold a dinner party on Wednesday of next week and told me to ask you if you feel capable of taking on the cooking. It's for eight people, including himself. He says if you don't feel up to it he will quite understand and get a chef from Oxford in as he usually does.'

Pandora looked at her uncle undecidedly. 'I don't know. What do you think?'

He shrugged. 'It's up to you, my dear. But you seem very capable to me.' He patted his stomach appreciatively. 'In fact I'd say you were almost as good as the chef from Oxford, and certainly a lot better than Mrs Symons, the housekeeper, who's done it once or twice when the chef hasn't been available.'

Pandora considered the idea a moment longer, then nodded. 'All right, I'll do it. Eight people isn't too many and I can always have at least one cold course which I can prepare beforehand.'

In fact she found it a challenge and began to take pleasure in working out the menu and ordering the ingredients to be sent out from a luxury store in Oxford. And even though she wouldn't admit it, she thoroughly enjoyed having the opportunity to use exotic and expensive foods that she had never been able to afford to cook before. Existence as a student meant ekeing out one's grant on the very cheapest of meals, and good food only came your way if you were lucky enough to have a rich boy-friend to pick up the tab occasionally.

'Who's coming to this dinner party anyway?' Pandora asked her uncle one morning just after the delivery from Oxford.

'Apart from Lady Townley, I have no idea,' he replied, picking at a fat bunch of grapes.

Pandora smacked his hand. 'Leave those alone, I need them. Who's Lady Townley?'

'I told you, Sir James' aunt. She always stays the night when she comes, so we'll have to get her room ready for her.' He paused to examine a carton of cream, then said, 'Though I'm surprised she's coming to such a small dinner party, and in the middle of the week. She usually only comes at weekends.'

The day before the dinner party, Uncle Charlie took her menu up to show Sir James and after a while he came back with the list of the wines he was to get from the cellar to go with it. There were almost as many types of wine as there were courses, and after running her eye over it Pandora decided that it wouldn't matter if the dessert turned out to be a hopeless failure anyway, because the guests would be too drunk to notice after getting through that little lot.

What with doing the cooking, helping to clean the

silver and wash the best crockery, preparing Lady
Townley's room, as well as all her usual jobs, Pandora
had no time at all to feel nervous, and as she had been
taught to be methodical she had everything well orga-
nised and actually had time to arrange the flowers that
the gardener had sent up on the afternoon of the party.
While she was doing so the door bell rang and Uncle
Charlie poked his head through the doorway of the
scullery.

'That will be Lady Townley. You'll have to come up
with me, Pandora, and take her things up to her room.'

Hastily she took off the coverall she had been wearing and ran up the steps behind him and through the
swing door into the entrance hall. As she did so Sir
James was hurrying down the last of the stairs and she
almost cannoned into him. He put out a hand to steady
her, catching hold of her arm. Pandora felt the strength
of his fingers through her sleeve, glanced up into his
face, muttered a suddenly breathless apology and
hastily pulled herself free of his grip.

Uncle Charlie had opened the door and Sir James
moved forward to greet his aunt, but Pandora looked at
the newcomer unseeingly for a few seconds until she
heard Sir James say, 'And this is Dora, our new maid,'
and she blinked and was able to focus again.

She found herself being regarded by a pair of lively
blue eyes set in a rather lived-in face, a face whose
owner enjoyed life to the full and didn't mind getting
older and showing it. The eyes twinkled at her suddenly
and Lady Townley smiled and nodded as if she had
satisfied herself about something. Pandora took her
coat and small suitcase up to her room and unpacked
for her while Uncle Charlie served her and Sir James tea
in the drawing room. Pandora smiled as she hung up

the older woman's evening dress, an elegantly simple
creation in grey silk; somehow she had the idea that
Lady Townley was far happier in the country tweeds
and serviceable shoes that she had arrived in rather
than this. She glanced round the room at the freshly
polished furniture and the vases of flowers, glad that
she had taken extra pains to make the room welcoming,
for there was something about Lady Townley that had
made Pandora take an instant liking for her.

The same instinct that had prompted her to take a
liking to Lady Townley made Pandora take an immediate dislike to another of the guests later that evening. She was again standing in the hall with Uncle
Charlie wearing her new black evening uniform dress
and little lace cap on her head, waiting to take the
women's wraps when they arrived and show them to the
cloakroom if necessary, and all the time worrying in case
the cleaning woman from the village, who had come in
to help for the evening, did something stupid and
ruined the main course that Pandora had left simmering
on the cooker. The first guests to arrive were two
middle-aged married couples who had travelled together, and Pandora had hardly finished hanging up
their coats before another car drew up and Uncle
Charlie ushered in Jonathan Thursby, the local vet she
had met at the stables. He smiled and came straight
over to her.

'Hallo again. I was hoping to see you tonight. You
haven't found life in the country too boring yet, then?'

Pandora smiled warmly back. 'No, I'm liking it more
than ever.'

'Good. Have you found out which day you're free
yet? That's if you'd really like to come on my rounds
with me, of course.'

Pandora hesitated for a second and then nodded. 'Yes, I would. Very much. And I'm free tomorrow, as a matter of fact.'

'Fine. Well, I have my morning surgery to do first, but I'm usually finished with that by ten-thirty. Suppose I pick you up about eleven, will that be okay?'

'Yes, that will be fine.'

'I'll look forward to seeing you, then.'

He smiled at her again, and then both of them became aware of a new arrival. They turned towards the doorway and found the last of the guests regarding them. It was a woman of about twenty-seven, tall and slimly elegant in a close-fitting black evening dress, her blonde hair cut fashionably short in a sleek head-hugging style, her face cleverly made up to accentuate her eyes and cheekbones. She was attractive, sophisticated and elegant—and she had the coldest eyes Pandora had ever seen.

Coolly she said, 'Hallo, Jon, how lovely to see you,' and held out a hand to him so that he had to leave Pandora and go and shake it, but the woman's eyes never left Pandora's face.

'Hallo, Cynthia. How are you?'

Pandora's eyes quickened with interest. So this was Cynthia Marsden, Sir James' mistress. Yes, she went with the clothes that she had proprietorially left in the closet upstairs. And she was the right type to be the mistress of a rich baronet—or to be his wife for that matter. Was there a marriage pending? she wondered. Or was Sir James the type who wouldn't marry when he could get what he wanted without it—or even *because* he could get what he wanted without it? Impossible to say one way or the other. At one time it was clear cut; a man just didn't marry his mistress, but nowadays it was an accepted fact that couples slept together before marriage, if they bothered to get married at all, but surely someone in Sir James' position . . .'

'Are you going to stand there staring all night, girl?'

Pandora hurried forward to take the mink stole that Cynthia Marsden thrust at her, although she had given no sign of waiting before.

'I'm so sorry.'

The older girl sniffed disdainfully. 'Really, servants these days are absolutely useless!' She turned and put a hand on Jon Thursby's arm. 'Where on earth did James dig that stupid little creature up from?' Then she smiled up at him. 'I haven't seen you for ages. You must be sure to tell me all about your pigs and cows and things.'

Uncle Charlie opened the door into the drawing room for them and they walked in together. Through the doorway Pandora saw Sir James look round and step forward to greet them. Immediately Cynthia let go of Jon's arm and stretched out her hands to her host, lifting up a laughing, glowing face for his kiss.

Pandora took the stole into the cloakroom and threw it viciously on to a chair. Trust that type of woman to have *real* fur, she wouldn't care how many poor little minks had to be killed just so that she could show off with her precious stole! She glared at it resentfully for a moment, then suddenly remembered the dinner and went running back to the kitchen with visions of disaster.

All was well, however, and the meal went without a hitch from the hors d'oeuvres to the home-made mints and stuffed dates. Afterwards she and Uncle Charlie more or less collapsed into a couple of chairs while their helper put the last of the pots and pans into the dishwasher and then went home.

'I think we deserve a drink,' he remarked, and poured her out a generous glass of the wine left over from the dinner party.

'Phew, I'm glad that's over. Are we finished now?'

'I'll have to go up to the drawing room again soon and replenish their drinks and then show them out when they leave.'

'What about Lady Townley, will she want anything?'

'She doesn't usually. She's very good and always tries to give as little trouble as possible.' Her uncle looked at her benignly and gave, for him, fulsome praise. 'You've worked hard the last couple of days and you did quite well tonight. If you're tired why don't you go on to bed; I'll get the women's wraps for them when they leave.'

'Thanks, but I think it's the heat in here and working over the stove as much as anything. I'll go and get some fresh air for a while.'

'All right, but they may not leave until the early hours of the morning and there's no point in us both sitting up.'

Pandora plonked him an affectionate kiss on the top of his head and went out through the yard and into the formal gardens at the front of the house. The sound of music and laughter came from the open windows of the drawing room and Pandora moved nearer the terrace so that she could see in. A record on the turntable was providing the background music while some of the guests sat around talking. At first she couldn't see Sir James and one of the couples, but then a light came on in the long gallery and she guessed that he was showing them round the house. Cynthia Marsden was sitting on a settee talking rather languidly with Jon Thursby, and Pandora wondered wryly if he was telling her about his 'pigs and cows and things'.

For an instant she felt a stab of something very like jealousy that she should be on the outside looking in and not a member of the party. But then she shrugged; such a staid party was hardly her thing, she and her friends at college were into disco dancing and all-night rock concerts at the moment. A dinner like tonight's was a parent-type non-event among her crowd. But even so her face was a little wistful as she continued to watch until Sir James and the remaining guests returned to the room. Cynthia Marsden, who had been looking openly bored, immediately became animated, looking up at Jon and laughing at something he had said, then she turned to her lover and held out her glass to him, but when he came to take it from her, got to her feet and stood close beside him, her arm through his. Just as if she owned him, Pandora thought cynically. Abruptly she turned away, feeling suddenly cold. How could a man let himself be used like that? She certainly hadn't expected Sir James to be the type who would let a woman walk all over him. But she supposed that men in love did silly things; even in her young life she had had boy-friends who had turned from being nice, sensible people into moody, besotted idiots when they thought they were in love with her.

She shivered in the chill air and hurried back to the house, but although she was tired she felt too restless to sleep and decided to go to the library to find herself something to read. Sir James seemed to have finished his tour of the house, and the library was far enough from the drawing room not to have any of the guests wandering in there. Her intention had been to find a comparatively modern novel that she could take back to her room to read, but as usual she couldn't resist examining some of the older books with their leather bindings and gold lettering, the pages often speckled brown with age. She ran her fingers lightly across the shelves, thinking that someone really ought to catalogue all these books and make sure that the more valuable ones were preserved from any damp that might be in the air. A very old-looking book caught her eyes, the title almost faded away, and she carefully drew it from its place. To her delight she found that it was a very early copy of Chaucer's *Troilus and Criseyde* and written in old English too.

Reverently Pandora carried her find to the chesterfield and made herself comfortable in its roomy depths, kicking off her shoes because her feet ached. For a couple of hours she read with avid enjoyment, but the beautiful old language was heavy going in places and gradually her head began to nod and she had to blink hard to keep awake. She yawned tiredly, but no way was she going to stop reading yet; she would lie in tomorrow on her day off. She read a few more pages but started to nod again. Perhaps if she just closed her eyes and rested them for a few minutes . . .

Something touched her face gently and she stirred, feeling cramped and cold. Slowly she opened her eyes. James Arbory was standing by the settee, looking down at her. Pandora blinked and hastily sat up, her book sliding off her lap down among the cushions of the chesterfield. Feeling totally confused, she reverted to her cockney accent and said, 'Oh, I—I must've dropped off.' Hastily she got to her feet.

'Do you make a habit of coming in here in the evenings, Dora?' he asked, his eyes noting her confusion.

'Oh, no, Sir James,' she lied, not wanting him to forbid her to use the room. 'I was just tidying up an' that, but I felt that tired, so I put me feet up for five minutes and must've gone off sound.'

'I see.' His expression was quite enigmatical, but somehow Pandora felt extremely uncomfortable, as if she was a mouse being played with by a cat.

'Can—can I go now, sir?'

'In a moment.' He moved to lean his shoulder against the high fireplace of white marble. For a moment he was silent, his expression unreadable, then he said surprisingly, 'Are you happy at Abbot's Arbory, Dora?'

'Oh yes. Yes, thank you.'

'And you think you'll stay with us for some time?'

She hesitated, knowing that she would be here only for the summer, but there was no point in telling him that. 'Yeah, I 'spose so,' she agreed.

'Good.' He straightened up and Pandora instinctively took a step backwards, but he seemed not to notice as he went on, 'I had intended to see you tomorrow to thank you for the way you cooked the meal tonight. It was faultless and everyone enjoyed it. You are to be congratulated.'

'Oh. Ta ever so,' she muttered awkwardly, hoping that he had finished and she would be able to leave.

But instead he went on, 'You must have had a great deal of practice to cook as well as that. Where did you learn?'

'I went to evening classes for a couple of years,' Pandora replied, glad to be able to be truthful for once.

'And have you never thought of taking up cooking for a living? There must be many opportunities.'

'No, I—I wouldn't want to be stuck in a kitchen all the time.' She looked at him pleadingly. 'I'm glad you enjoyed me cookin', but can I go now, sir? I'm really ever so tired.'

'Yes, of course. Goodnight, Dora.'

'G'night, sir.'

She hurried from the room and down the corridor towards the servants' quarters, and it wasn't until the tiled floors struck cold to her feet that she remembered that she had left her shoes in the library. Well, never mind, she could get them in the morning. But then she remembered the copy of Chaucer she had been reading and stopped, appalled that she could have treated a valuable book in such a way. Why, the pages might get bent or even come away from the backing if she left it there all night. Damn! It was all Sir James' fault. Why did he have to come to the library at this hour of night? He should have been safely tucked up in bed with the glamorous Cynthia by now.

Looking at her watch, she decided to give Sir James twenty minutes in which to leave the library and go to his room, or whoever's room he was going to, and then she would slip back to the library and replace the book and collect her shoes. The time passed with intolerable slowness, but at last the twenty minutes were up and Pandora made her way back, her bare feet making no noise on the oak floor. Softly she turned the handle and pushing the door open stepped into the room. Then stopped abruptly. Sir James was still there, standing by the fireplace with a book in his hands, slowly turning the pages. It was the copy of *Troilus and Criseyde* that she had been reading!

He looked up from the book. With cold firmness he said, 'Yes, Dora, I think you'd better come in—and shut the door behind you.'

CHAPTER FIVE

SLOWLY Pandora obeyed. She opened her mouth to speak, but Sir James cut in, 'And please don't insult my intelligence again by using that phoney accent. You're not a good enough actress to keep it up indefinitely.'

She flushed; he certainly wasn't pulling his punches. But she said calmly enough, 'I forgot my shoes.'

He glanced down at her feet, then his eyes came back to her face, probing. 'And I don't think that's all you forgot, was it?'

It took a great effort of will not to look at the book in his hands, but she managed to keep her eyes on his face as she tried to bluff it out and answered, 'No, there was only my shoes.'

His mouth thinned. 'And this? I suppose you just happened to pick it up.'

'That old book? I must have been dusting it when I . . .' Her voice trailed away as she saw his eyes narrow and a dangerous glint come into them.

'Yes,' he said softly, menacingly, 'it's much wiser of you not to try to lie to me. I don't like little girls who tell lies, and you're as bad at that as you are at keeping up a common accent.' He put the book down carefully on a side table and took a couple of steps towards her. 'I think you owe me an explanation. You're no common little ignoramus, Dora, so why the big act?'

Pandora hesitated, wondering how much she could manage to hide from him. One thing was certain, though, whatever she said she mustn't implicate Uncle Charlie. But maybe she was a better actress than Sir

James surmised. So she opened her eyes wide and said rather tremblingly, 'I'm sorry if I've deceived you, Sir James, but you see I really only wanted a job for the summer, but I went to several agencies and they all said they only had permanent vacancies and said I was more suited to office work. But I . . .'

'Just a moment,' James Arbory interrupted. 'Why did you only want a summer job?'

'Well, because . . . as a matter of fact I'm a student and I just needed to work until the end of my vacation.'

'I thought as much,' he said on a note of satisfaction. 'I knew that voice could never go with that face.'

Pandora blinked, then went on hurriedly, 'But I wanted to work in the country and I needed a live-in job, so I—well, I'm afraid I lied and said I was free to take on a long-term position, and I used the cockney accent because they all seemed to think I ought to do office work. But as soon as I spoke like that I got this domestic job at once.'

She looked at him hopefully, wondering if she had got away with it, and to her relief she saw a look of amusement on his face.

'I see. Very enterprising.' He put his hands in the pockets of his black evening suit and moved nearer to sit on the edge of a big mahogany desk. 'So you're a student. Where?'

'At London University.'

'And what are you studying?'

Reluctantly she answered, 'For my B.A. I hope to become a librarian.'

His left eyebrow rose in surprise. 'So that's why you were looking at the Chaucer. Can you read it?'

Pandora's chin came up. 'Yes, I can read it.'

A mocking look came into his eyes. 'Brains, beauty

and cooking too. Is there no end to your talents, Dora?'

Two bright spots of colour came into her cheeks and she said uncertainly, 'You just said I was a terrible actress.'

'Oh, yes.' The mockery deepened. 'But sometimes that can be a distinct advantage.'

'It—it can?' Pandora found that she was stammering, her pulses racing.

'Mm. Especially at moments like this.' Unhurriedly he straightened up and took his hands from his pockets. Then he moved to stand close to her and almost casually put his hand on her waist and drew her towards him. His arms went round her and for a moment he looked down into her face, her green eyes wide and startled. 'Yes, definitely at moments like this,' he murmured softly, then bent to kiss her.

His mouth was firm and hard against hers, his lips insinuating as they explored her mouth with little kisses that promised but didn't satisfy. Pandora's mouth moved under his. She tried to pull away, gasping, 'No! No, please,' but his hand came up to coil itself in her hair and he forced her head back. His mouth became more demanding and suddenly Pandora's head started to whirl. She felt the strangest sensations; as if the room was spinning round and she was sinking down, down into a deep whirlpool. She gave a little moan, her mouth opening. His lips moved against hers, sensuous, exploring. Desire grew deep inside her, slowly at first but then with gathering momentum, until she was filled with longing, an aching need for fulfilment. She wanted to move closer to him, to put her arms round his neck and to return his kiss, to let passion take over. But some instinct for self-preservation held her back and she stood still in his arms, not fighting him but not returning his embrace.

At last he lifted his head and Pandora slowly opened her eyes. He was looking down at her quizzically, awaiting her reaction. She fought to regain her composure, but even so her voice was still unsteady as she said coldly, 'Do you always take advantage of your female servants?'

The ghost of a smile curved his lips. 'Only when they're as young and as incredibly lovely as you.'

Pandora felt the colour heighten in her cheeks. How on earth did she reply to such fulsome flattery as that? Abruptly she pulled away from him. 'Let go of me!'

Unhurriedly he took his hands away, watching her with the same quirk to his lips, as if he found the whole thing extremely amusing. Anger filled her and she said scathingly, 'You're about three hundred years out of date, aren't you? The droit du seigneur thing went out with the Middle Ages. Or hadn't you heard? Nowadays people don't have to put up with that sort of treatment.'

The amused curve deepened. 'So what are you going to do about it?'

Pandora's fists clenched at her sides. 'Leave, of course,' she answered shortly.

James Arbory put his hand on her neck and gently caressed her throat with his thumb. Pandora's heart began to race and it took every ounce of strength she had not to tremble at his touch. 'No, you won't leave,' he said softly.

She tried to open her mouth, to say that she would, but his fingers burned into her skin and somehow the words stuck in her throat.

A little gleam of triumph came into his eyes, and he moved a little nearer to her. 'No,' he repeated, 'you won't leave, Dora, because you want this as much as I do,' and he drew her unresistingly close to kiss her again.

This time when he let her go she kept her head lowered, reluctant to look at him and see that light of triumph again in his eyes. For a few moments he didn't speak, then he said rather thickly, 'You'll stay?'

Slowly, reluctantly, she nodded.

His hand gripped her shoulder suddenly, hurting her as he stared down at her bent head. Then he let go abruptly. His voice suddenly harsh, James Arbory said, 'What a child you are!' He stepped away from her towards the fireplace, reaching up a hand to grip the mantelshelf. For a long moment he looked at her moodily, then he gave an impatient sort of shrug and said, 'You must be tired, why don't you go to bed?'

His sudden change of mood threw her and for a moment Pandora could only stare at him, then she hurriedly bent to pick up her shoes and slip them on. She gave him a last quick glance, but he was gazing down into the empty fireplace, a frown between his brows, so she turned and hurried to the door, closing it gently behind her before running down the long corridors to her room, running as if all the devils in hell were behind her.

But the sanctuary of her room provided little peace of mind; she realised that by submitting to James Arbory's masculine domination, even so little as she had, she had made an absolute fool of herself. The only sensible thing to do now would be to leave first thing in the morning, before anyone was about. She could leave a note for Uncle Charlie with some excuse, say a friend had found her a job—anything! Anything, so long as she got away from Abbot's Arbory and away from its master! She shivered, knowing that if she stayed here a minute longer than necessary she would be placing herself even deeper under his domination. Pandora had been kissed many times by various boy-friends, but never before had her senses been so immediately stirred, her emotions roused so that she was in danger of losing control. The moment he had begun to kiss her she had found herself wanting to submit to a sexual mastery that had almost overwhelmed her, only the strongest effort of will making her hold back from surrendering herself to him completely.

Feverishly she picked up a pen and scrabbled round in her bag for a piece of paper. She got as far as writing 'Dear Uncle Charlie,' and then stopped, the pen poised over the paper. Slowly she put it down and sank down on to the bed. It was no good, Sir James had been right all along; she had wanted him to kiss her—and more, much more than that. She shivered again uncontrollably. Even though she had resisted him, he had known that she was his. It had been like an electric shock running through her, making every nerve in her body tingle and come alive, and she could no more run away from a man who was capable of rousing her like that than she could swim the channel or fly to the moon. She was on terribly dangerous ground and she knew it, there was every chance of getting her fingers badly burned, but she just *had* to stay, even if only to see whether she had the strength of mind to resist him completely when he tried it again. And that he would try to seduce her again, Pandora was quite, quite certain.

Jonathan Thursby called for her promptly at eleven the next morning. He was driving a blue estate car that had a metal grille between the back seats and the boot. 'In case I ever have to transport any tigers back to the surgery,' he told her jokingly as he helped her into the passenger seat.

'Our first stop had better be to check on Greymist, I think,' he said as he joined her in the car.

'Why, is something wrong with her?'

'No, but I like to keep my eye on her, so as I'm here I thought I'd drop in.'

They walked together into the stableyard and across to Greymist's box. The mare whickered with pleasure and blew softly down her nostrils as Pandora stroked her head.

Jon laughed. 'I see you've made a conquest. It's obviously the feminine touch that does it. I'd ask you to hold her head for me while I look her over, but I've an idea Mr Langley would have a fit if I did.' He looked around. 'I'd better go and find him; he really shouldn't leave the stables unattended like this. These are valuable horses.'

He walked off towards Mr Langley's house and Pandora slipped Greymist the lumps of sugar she had brought with her. 'Yes, you're a beauty, aren't you?' she cooed to the horse as it tossed its mane. 'But it doesn't matter how haughtily you behave, you know I'll always bring . . .'

'Dora.'

Her heart lurched and she jumped so much that the horse shied away nervously. Pulses racing crazily, she turned to face the speaker, but then gave a little gasp of relief as she saw that it was only Tom Langley.

'Oh, you—you startled me!'

'I've been up to the house looking for you, but Mr Richardson said it was your day off and that you'd gone out. The way he said it I thought he meant you'd gone right away from the estate. I didn't realise you'd only come over here to look for me. We must have missed each other on the way.'

Pandora shook her head. 'I didn't come to see you, Tom, I only came to . . .'

He came up to her, a cocky grin on his face. 'Come off it, you don't really think I believe that line about coming to see the horses, do you?'

'Why not? It's true,' Pandora replied, looking at him steadily.

For a moment he looked disconcerted, but then his natural vanity reasserted itself and he said, 'You don't have to play games; I'm not the type who thinks a girl's cheap just because she encourages a man. Why waste time pretending to be a prude when we could *really* be getting to know one another?'

Pandora looked at him exasperatedly; how on earth did you get through a king-sized ego like that? She supposed he was a little older than she, about twenty-two or three, and he was quite good-looking except that his hair was too long and greasy and there were pockmarks on his cheeks. Not that he could help that, of course, but he smelt of horses and he didn't clean his nails properly. Pandora guessed that he was one of the local young bucks and probably had all the girls in the village trailing after him, so that he was able to pick and choose. And he now expected her to be the same, to fall into his lap when he crooked his little finger. Pandora smiled mirthlessly to herself; like master, like man. Did all the men in the country see themselves as God's gift to town girls? Well, this one at least she definitely could resist.

Coldly she answered, 'Mr Thursby is here. He's gone to find your father.'

Tom swore. 'What the hell does he want to do that for? Now I'll get into a row for leaving the stables.' He started to hurry towards the house. 'Thanks for giving me the tip, Dora. I'll thank you properly some other time.' He winked at her and went to pat her bottom as he passed, but Pandora moved adroitly out of the way.

He came back about five minutes later with Jon and his father, and it was obvious from their conversation that he had lied his way out of trouble. He gave her a triumphant wink which Pandora ignored, trying to show him by her attitude that she disliked him, but somehow she had a feeling that she was just wasting her time.

Jon looked the mare over while Mr Langley held her head, and pronounced himself well satisfied.

'She's doing fine. As long as she doesn't get frightened or upset so that the foal comes prematurely, she'll be all right.' He turned to smile at Pandora. 'So let's get on our way, shall we?' He put a hand under her elbow and nodded to Mr Langley. 'I'll call again in a few days' time, but if you're at all worried about her in the meantime give me a ring, day or night.'

He led Pandora towards his waiting car and she saw with some satisfaction the indignant look on Tom Langley's face. Perhaps *now* he would get the message.

Their next stop was at a farm where Jon had to examine a couple of cows in a field near the farmhouse. Pandora sat on a gate and watched until the farmer's wife, unable to curb her curiosity any longer, came to ask her in for a cup of tea and tried to find out who she was and what her relationship was to Jon. Pandora evaded the questions as best she could without being downright rude, but was glad when Jon came in and she could jump up and signal urgently with her eyebrows at him not to accept the cup of tea he was offered.

He washed his hands and then joined her in the car. 'What was all that about?' he asked as he drove away.

'That woman at the farm; she kept asking me all sorts of questions.'

'What about?'

'About me, and—well, about you *and* me, if you see what I mean.'

Jon grinned. 'Oh, sure, I see all right. Sorry, I suppose I should have thought of that. I've never taken a girl with me on my rounds before, you see.'

'So I gathered,' Pandora returned drily. 'That woman wouldn't happen to be the local gossip by any chance, would she?' And when Jon nodded rather shamefacedly, she groaned and added, 'And now I suppose it will be all over the area that I'm your girl-friend or something.'

He glanced across at her. 'Would you mind that much?'

His tone was casual enough, but there was something in his voice that stopped Pandora from laughing as she had been about to and instead answer lightly, 'It wouldn't be true, would it?'

'But it could quite easily be, if you wanted it.'

She sat silently for a long moment, then said slowly, 'Jon, we've only just met and I—quite honestly I don't know what I want. So, please, don't let's get involved, okay?'

He smiled ruefully. 'Okay. I always was the slow, plodding type anyway.'

Pandora laughed at him. 'I'm sure you're not. Where are we going next?'

'To visit an old-age pensioner in a village a couple of miles farther on. He's got something wrong with his dog.'

They continued on the round with Pandora helping where she could and she found it intensely interesting, but there were times, particularly when they were driving from place to place, when she fell silent and became absorbed in her own thoughts. Jon looked at her, won-

dering if he were the cause, and would have been cha-
grined if he had known that they were not of him but of
James Arbory. Again and again she went back to that
scene in the library last night, remembering the way he
had kissed her, the pressure of his mouth on hers, the
heat that had seared through her body like a flame. She
stirred in her seat, lips parted softly, her eyes far
away—only coming back to an awareness of her surroundings again when she realised that Jon had pulled
up and was looking at her searchingly.

'Dora? Are you all right?'

She flushed, acutely embarrassed and said hastily,
'Yes, I'm fine, really. It's just that—oh, nothing. I was
just thinking about my job, wondering whether I'll stay
there.'

His eyebrows rose. 'Aren't you happy?'

Pandora shrugged. 'I don't think it's my scene.'

He smiled at her choice of words, but then became
serious as he reached out and took her hand. 'Well, I
hope you do decide to stay, Dora, very much.
Especially as we've just started to get to know one
another.'

Looking up at him, Pandora felt suddenly ashamed;
he was so open and friendly that her masquerade
seemed cheap and childish. Impulsively she covered his
hand with her other one and said, 'Look, Jon, I'm
afraid I haven't been altogether straight with you. I
never intended to stay at Abbot's Arbory later than
September anyway. You see, I'm a student and I just
wanted a job for the summer, but I couldn't very well
tell Sir James that when he employed me. And my name
isn't Dora, it's Pandora.'

Jon looked at her in some astonishment, then said,
'But why, if you went to so much trouble to get the job,

think of leaving when you've only been there two or three weeks?'

'Because yesterday I had to tell Sir James the truth. He—he may not want me to stay now.'

'I see.' He thought for a minute and then said, 'Well, look, if he does decide to get rid of you, I can always use an assistant in my practice; looking after the animals at the surgery and that kind of thing. And as you seem to have such a way with animals I'm sure you'd be good at the job, and enjoy it too.'

Pandora looked at him gratefully. 'Thanks, Jon, I really appreciate the offer, but I'm sure you don't really need anyone, and I just couldn't impose on your kindness like that.'

'Nonsense, all the animal owners for miles around will come flocking to the surgery with you as a receptionist.'

She smiled but shook her head.

'Well, keep it in mind. The offer stays open as long as you want it.' He leaned forward and lifted her chin to look into her face. 'And I hope you'll accept, because I don't want to lose you as soon as I've found you, Pandora.'

He moved his head nearer as if he was going to kiss her, but she lowered her eyes and turned her head away.

After a moment he took his hand off hers and sat up. In a rather gruff voice, he said, 'Maybe we'd better be going.'

He drove her round to the tradesmen's entrance of the house and cut off her thanks abruptly.

'It was my pleasure. Will you come out with me again?'

She nodded. 'Yes, I'd like to.'

He reached out and gripped her hand. 'And you

won't leave without letting me know? Promise me that, Pandora.'

For a moment she hesitated, but the earnest entreaty in his face made her nod, albeit rather reluctantly. 'Yes, all right, I promise.'

'Good. I'll give you a ring later in the week.'

Pandora had to square her shoulders to go into the house, wondering whether Sir James was at home and if he would ring for her on some excuse and try to kiss her again. But most of all she wondered whether this time she would have the strength to resist him.

But almost as soon as she entered the kitchen, Uncle Charlie informed her that their employer was leaving first thing in the morning to travel to Ireland where he hoped to purchase some new stallions and would be away for a week or so. Pandora's first feeling was one of relief, but it was one that didn't last; almost at once she realised that it had only postponed the inevitable and that now she would have to wait in apprehensive suspense for his return.

Life at Abbot's Arbory was quiet with its master away, almost as if the heart and purpose had gone out of it. Pandora and Uncle Charlie were able to get up later and eat at times to suit themselves instead of fitting in around Sir James, and now she didn't have to keep an ear cocked for his footsteps while she was cleaning so that she could slip away and avoid him. She had more free time too, but spent it more in solitary walks round the park with just the dogs for company rather than going to the stables where she would inevitably run into Tom Langley. It was annoying that the pleasure she derived from the horses should be curtailed because of his unwanted attentions, but it was also pleasant to be entirely alone for a while after living

at college where there were always people around her
all through the day and where she had to share a room
with another girl, so that solitude became a thing to be
treasured.

But her attempts to rid herself of Tom Langley
proved fruitless, for he came every day to seek her out
at the house, waiting—much to Uncle Charlie's annoyance—in the kitchen until she put in an appearance,
and no amount of hints or even downright rudeness
would get rid of him. That he had a crush on her he
made evident, and he was always on at her to go out
with him to the cinema, or 'the flicks', as he called it.
Pandora found no difficulty at all in refusing, but he
was convinced that she was only playing hard to get
and that he only had to keep on asking for her to eventually give in.

During the following week Pandora had another day
out with Jon which she enjoyed, mostly because he was
wise enough to keep the conversation to impartial
topics and not again mention his liking for her. This
time she consented to go back with him to the nearby
market town of Broxford where he had his surgery and
see the animals that he was caring for personally.
Afterwards they sat round a log fire and ate toasted
crumpets oozing with butter and drank mugs of cocoa
while they listened to some of Jon's collection of clas-
sical records. It was fun, and to Pandora held no great
importance because that was the kind of thing she and
her friends did in each other's rooms all the time.
Perhaps to Jon it held more significance, but if it did he
was clever enough not to let it show, but the local gos-
sips had a field day. News of her day out with Jon earlier had already gone the rounds, and as it was the kind
of small town where everybody knew everyone else's

business better than their own, it was soon common knowledge that the new maid at Abbot's Arbory had spent several hours alone with Jon in his house at night and that she must, therefore, be highly immoral.

No one, of course, mentioned this in Jon's hearing, and it never even occurred to Pandora that rumours might be going round about her, but it soon came to Tom Langley's ears and he descended on the kitchen in an indignant rage.

'What's this I hear about you going out with the vet?' he demanded, a scowl on his face.

Pandora looked at him exasperatedly. 'What do you mean?'

'You know darn well what I mean. Do you fancy him or something?'

'Not particularly, no,' Pandora answered as she turned to put some dishes in the cupboard.

'Why go out with him, then?'

'Because I wanted to, of course.' Then she added more placatingly because she didn't want to row, 'It was interesting going on his rounds with him and seeing the type of work a country vet has to do.'

'I could have borrowed my dad's car and taken you for a drive round the country, if that's what you wanted,' he told her belligerently.

'It would hardly be the same,' Pandora pointed out.

'No, it wouldn't, would it?' he returned angrily. 'Don't think I don't know why you went out with him. It's because he's what they call one of the professional classes. You're just trying to get off with him for what you can get out of him. You town girls are all the same—always going for the bloke who'll spend the most money on them.'

'That isn't true!' retorted Pandora indignantly.

'Then why go out with him instead of me, if you don't fancy him?'

'I've already told you ...' she began, but he interrupted her with a derisive snort.

'Yagh, don't give me all that country vet stuff. I wasn't born yesterday, you know. You're just a snob, Dora. You don't think I'm good enough for you, do you? Why go out with the bloke who mucks out the stables when you can go out with the vet?'

'That isn't so at all,' Pandora answered, shocked that he should think such a thing of her when she had always prided herself on her indifference to class distinction.

'Prove it, then. Come out with me as well as Mr Thursby.'

'All right, if that's the only thing that will convince you, I will,' she retorted before she had had time to think, then groaned inwardly as she saw the triumphant grin on his face and realised she had walked straight into his trap.

'Good, we'll go tonight,' he told her, pushing home his victory. 'I'll borrow Dad's car and pick you up at half past six to go to the flicks. There's an *Emanuelle* film on; you'll like that. And we'll go for a drink after. See, I don't mind how much money I spend on a girl either. And I bet I give you a better time than that snotty vet does, too.' He gave her a cocky wave as he went out of the door. 'See you later, darlin'.'

Pandora grimaced. *Now* what had she let herself in for? But that thrust about her being a snob had cut home. *Was* that why she preferred Jon? She sighed; well, it was too late now, if she tried to get out of it Tom would make life unbearable, so she would just have to endure the evening as best she could.

But right from the start he assumed an arrogant, swaggering manner and bought her a big box of chocolates she didn't want in an attempt to impress her. The film frankly made her blush, but she was too taken up with stopping Tom trying to kiss her and to prevent his hands groping her to give it too much attention. After the film she refused point blank to go to a pub, reckoning that he would be even more difficult to handle after he had had a few drinks, and told him that she wanted to go home. Fortunately, but surprisingly, he didn't argue and they set off back to Abbot's Arbory in silence.

Pandora began to relax, her mind on other things, but came to with a jerk when she realised that Tom had turned the car off the main road into an overgrown lane and pulled into the entrance of a farm track.

He switched off the engine and turned to her with a lascivious grin. '*Now* we can really start to enjoy ourselves. Let's get in the back seat.'

'Wait a minute, Tom Langley. If you think you're going to get anything from me, you're mistaken. So you can just turn this car round and take me home!'

'Aw, come on, Dora, stop playing hard to get. You know you're hot for it.' He reached out to pull her towards him, his hand searching for the buttons of her blouse.

Pandora pushed him violently away. 'For heaven's sake! Doesn't anything get through that thick head of yours? I don't fancy you, Tom. Now leave me alone!'

'Come off it. Everyone knows you're a tart. If you can do it for Jonathan Thursby you can do it for me.' And again he reached for her, catching her wrist and jerking her towards him while his free hand pulled up her skirt.

'Let go of me!' Pandora balled her hand into a fist and punched him in the mouth as he tried to kiss her.

'You bitch! I'll make you pay for that.' He bent her arm back so that she gave a cry of pain and grabbed a handful of her hair, pulling her head up so that she couldn't get away when he put his mouth on hers. Vainly she tried to get free, but he was as strong as one of the horses he cared for, and he was enjoying hurting her when she struggled.

At last Pandora realised that there was only one way she was going to get out of this situation and she suddenly relaxed, pretending to acquiesce and let him kiss her.

'All right, you win,' she told him when he lifted his head. 'We *will* go in the back seat.'

He laughed insolently and squeezed her breast. '*Now* you're talking! I knew you were hot stuff the minute I set eyes on you. And don't worry, I'll satisfy you more than Jonathan Thursby ever could, you'll see.'

He got out of the car and opened the back door, Pandora picking up her bag and following more slowly. Then, as soon as he was inside the car, she slammed the door on her side and began to run down the lane back towards the main road. There was a furious shout and then the sound of heavy footsteps thundering along behind her. Pandora reached the more open main road and turned left in the direction of Arbory Magna, still running as hard as she could and hoping that either Tom would give up or else a car would come along that she could flag down. But there were no cars and he kept on coming, until Pandora realised with sickening dread that he was gaining on her. His outdoor life and manual work probably kept him fit, while a long winter in college had made her out of condition. Her only chance was to hide and hope that he wouldn't find her, so she ran on to the grass verge, looking for a place to hide, although it was difficult to see in the near blackness. But maybe she could use that to help her. Panting heavily, she came to a clump of trees that looked as if there might be more trees behind them, plunged away from the road and ran in between them, trying to make as little noise as possible. After about thirty yards or so she found a tree with fairly low branches and sprang up, swinging herself on to it and then quickly climbing higher among the concealing foliage of the leaves. She sat astride a branch, clinging to the tree trunk, and trying to control the hammering of her heart and her sobbing, gasping breath.

She heard Tom coming into the wood, searching for her, muttering curses as he stumbled over a root. He came nearer and Pandora hardly dared to breathe, biting her lip hard in case he heard her. He paused almost under the tree, listening, and then she realised that she had lost her bag. Her heart froze; had he found it beneath the tree? Was that why he was standing there, looking up into the branches for her?

But then he moved on, cursing again, and soon after he began to call for her. 'Dora! Stop being so silly. It's all right, you can come out. I'm not going to do anything. If you come out I'll take you home.'

Humph, if she believed that she'd believe anything.

He searched around for her for another ten minutes or so and then he shouted out, 'All right then, damn you! You can stay here all night for all I care! You little slut!' He passed near her tree again on his way back to the road and then she heard him walk along the tarmac surface until his footsteps receded into the distance. Ten minutes later she heard a car go by in the direction of Arbory Magna and gave a sigh of relief, but even so she stayed on her uncomfortable perch for another twenty minutes; it just might have been a different car that had gone by and Tom was still waiting on the road for her to come out.

For this reason, too, when she did climb down Pandora kept among the trees as she walked parallel to the road for another half a mile before venturing on to the better surface. She judged that she must be at least five miles from Abbot's Arbory, and the shoes she was wearing were definitely not designed for five-mile hikes. Still, she supposed she was lucky to have got off so lightly, things could so easily have gone the other way, so she would just have to put up with it and serve her right for having gone out with Tom in the first place.

She had been going for about half a mile when she heard the sound of a car coming up behind her. For a second she felt fear in case it was Tom and looked wildly round for somewhere to hide, but then she realised that this engine was a soft purr in comparison to Tom's rather noisy one, and hopefully put up her thumb in the hope of getting a lift. The car, a big, sleek job, passed by and she turned to walk on with a sigh, but then it came to a sudden stop a few yards down the road.

Pandora ran to it eagerly and opened the passenger door. 'Oh, please, can you give me a lift to . . .' and then broke off as she found herself staring at Cynthia Marsden, and sitting beside her in the driver's seat, an angry frown on his face, was James Arbory.

'I thought it was you. Get in,' he ordered grimly.

Reluctantly Pandora obeyed him and got into the back seat, although she had a feeling that it might have been better to walk the whole way home on bleeding and blistered feet!

CHAPTER SIX

SIR JAMES started the car again and drove on in silence, but Pandora could feel his anger; it hung in the car like something tangible. Presumably because he had wanted to be alone with his girl-friend and had felt obliged to stop and pick her up, Pandora supposed.

She sat quietly, trying to efface herself, but Cynthia Marsden half turned in her seat to look at her. 'Do you always hitch lifts home—Dorothy, isn't it?'

'No, it's Dora. I missed the bus,' Pandora muttered, unwilling to let the older woman get an even bigger rise out of her.

'Really? I thought the last bus didn't leave until midnight. Doesn't it, darling?' she asked, addressing Sir James.

'I've no idea,' he replied curtly.

Pandora looked up and found his eyes, dark with anger, on her in the driving mirror. For a long moment their glances locked and then he lowered his eyes to watch the road again. She turned away, feeling strangely empty and confused, and saw that Cynthia Marsden was staring at her in scarcely contained fury, and realised with a sickening feeling that she had seen.

The other girl's lips set into a thin hard line and Pandora could almost see her inner struggle to contain her rage, then, after a minute or so, she said in a silky voice, 'Why, Dora, your jacket is covered in dirt.'

Glancing down at her sleeves, Pandora saw that they, and the front of her coat, were stained with moss from the trunk of the tree she had climbed. Her skirt, too, was streaked with it and had a jagged tear. Rather hollowly she said, 'I tripped and fell.'

'Good heavens! It looks more as if you've been rolling around on the ground,' Cynthia returned, her tone heavy with implication. 'Did you spend the evening in Broxford?'

'Yes, at the cinema.'

'Oh, that place where they show all the explicit sex films,' Cynthia said disdainfully, for all the world as if she herself was as white as the driven snow.

She opened her mouth to make some other remark, but the car stopped with rather a jerk outside a neat Georgian house standing a little way back from the road, that Pandora recognised as being on the outskirts of Arbory Magna. So this was where Cynthia Marsden lived. How convenient!

The older girl immediately turned her attention on Sir James. 'You are coming in for a nightcap, aren't you, darling? I'm sure your maid can walk from here.'

'Yes, of course I can.' Pandora moved to open the door, but James Arbory said curtly, 'Wait,' then got out to open Cynthia's door for her. He walked with her up the driveway to the house and after a few moments a light came on inside.

Pandora bit her lip, wondering whether to get out and walk the rest of the way as she would very much like to do, but was afraid that it would make her employer even angrier if he came out and found her gone. But if Cynthia succeeded in her obvious intention to keep him with her he might be ages, hours even, if they got really involved. But he surprised her by coming back within a couple of minutes, getting into the car and driving away immediately. He drove decorously through the sleeping village, but put his foot down so that the powerful car seemed to surge up the hill, the trees flicking past as darker shadows in the night. At the sound of his horn someone came running to open the gates and then they were through and speeding down the mile-long drive to the waiting house. He pulled up so sharply outside the entrance that gravel sprayed up from the tyres. Then he got out and jerked her door open.

Pandora hastily scrambled out. 'Thank you for the lift.' She started towards the side entrance, but Sir James reached out and caught her arm.

'Oh, no, you don't. I want a word with you.'

His grip like a vice, he propelled her up the steps and through the big double doors, kicking them shut behind him. Then he half dragged her down the corridor and into the drawing room. Only then, when he had shut the door, did he let her go.

'Now,' he said furiously, 'you're going to tell me what the hell you were doing thumbing a lift at this time of night.'

Pandora automatically began to rub her arm where he had held it. 'I told you, I missed the . . .' Her voice faded as she saw the sudden flame of rage in his eyes and she took a hasty step backwards, but he reached out and caught her wrist.

'Yes, it would be much wiser if you didn't lie to me,' he said silkily, menacingly.

Her eyes went to his hand circling her wrist, biting into her flesh, and then she raised them to his face and began to tremble.

'Well?' he demanded.

'I—I was out on a date. And he—well, he got over-amorous, so I got out of his car to walk home.'

'And the dirt on your clothes?' He indicated her stained jacket.

'He came after me,' Pandora admitted reluctantly. 'I ran in a wood to hide, but it wasn't very thick and I had to shin up a tree so he wouldn't find me.'

'And then he drove off and left you to walk home alone, I suppose?' Sir James said grimly. 'And did it never occur to you that by thumbing a lift you might run into the same danger again? That someone else might have tried to have sex with you?'

Pandora shook her head and said rather helplessly, 'My feet hurt.'

He raised his eyes to heaven. 'Dear God!' He looked at her again and his face hardened. 'Who was it, Dora? Some lout from the village?'

She hesitated; although she had no reason to protect Tom Langley after tonight, she was reluctant to get him into trouble because she knew that it was bound to upset his parents, both of whom she liked very much. She had received nothing but kindness from them, especially from Mr Langley, who had let her help groom the horses, and she didn't want to be the one to bring trouble on Tom, who was their only child and the apple of their eyes—and spoiled rotten because of it, she realised.

So she lied and said, 'No, it was someone I met in Oxford.'

His eyes narrowed. 'Is that the truth?'

She nodded, 'Yes,' and lowered her head to avoid his scrutiny.

'Because if it's not ...' he began threateningly, his fingers tightening on her wrist as he pulled her towards him.

Looking up, she saw the dark flame in his eyes and

involuntarily whispered, 'No!' But it was as if he hadn't heard; he drew her close against him, one hand low on her hips so that she felt the lean hardness of his body. He bent his head and sought her lips, his kiss soft, sensuous. Only for a moment did she put up a token resistance and then her mouth opened under his and her arms crept round his neck. He kissed her eyes, her throat, sending sensations of delight running through her. She moved against him and could feel the growing tension in his body as he bit the lobe of her ear. Then his lips were on her mouth again, but hard now and demanding. She responded passionately, eagerly, and made no demur when he slipped off her jacket and it fell to the ground. His fingers sought the buttons of her blouse and that, too, fell to the floor, then his hands were cupping her breasts, his thumbs exploring, caressing. Pandora moaned softly, her mouth moving under his. He lifted his head and stared at her for a moment, his breath ragged and uneven, then he stooped to pick her up and carry her to one of the large, deep settees, laying her gently down on its cushioned softness.

He sat down on the edge, feasting his eyes on her youthful loveliness, then he reached out and began to caress her again so that her breasts hardened beneath his fingers. Pandora writhed and moaned, then opened eyes grown dark as jade by desire and lifted her arms to pull his head down, so that his lips, too, could kiss and caress her, holding his head there as wave after wave of desire ran through her, making her groan and bury her fingers in his hair. Then he was lying beside her on the settee, murmuring her name over and over again, and kissing her with a fierce, hungry passion.

Pandora didn't know how long it was that they lay together, until he suddenly pushed himself away and got to his feet, standing with his back to her. 'You'd better get dressed,' he said abruptly, his voice harsh and uneven.

Slowly she sat up, looking at him rather dazedly, unable yet to fully comprehend what had happened. She pushed her hair back out of her eyes with shaking fingers, then looked round for her things.

'Here.' He picked up her blouse from the floor and tossed it to her, giving her only a glance before turning away again.

She held the blouse against her, covering herself as she stared at his broad back, then she slowly swung her legs to the floor and with fumbling hands put it on and did up the buttons while he went to the sideboard to pour himself a glass of Scotch. Getting up, she crossed to pick up her jacket and started for the door, but he said urgently, 'No, wait!' and she slowly turned to look back at him.

His hair was dishevelled, his grey eyes still shadowed by unfulfilled passion. For a few moments he studied her as she stood waiting, then he put down the glass and moved forward to put his hands on her shoulders. 'Goodnight, Dora. My beautiful girl,' he said gently.

She looked up at him wonderingly, bewildered by his change of mood. Slowly she said, 'Goodnight, Sir James.'

He shook his head. 'Goodnight, *James*,' he corrected her, his eyes warm.

Softly she repeated it. 'Goodnight—James.'

He smiled, then bent to kiss her, his mouth gentle. 'Go now. I'll see you tomorrow.'

Pandora went to the door and opened it. She looked back at him standing so tall and powerful, the master of Arbory, and then at the settee. Her eyes flew to meet his

and then she quietly shut the door and walked slowly
through the moonlit corridors of the great house to her
room.

It was late the next morning before Pandora woke,
and for once she didn't spring out of bed immediately
as she usually did, but lay languidly gazing up at the
shaft of sunlight that lay along the ceiling from the gap
in the curtains. She knew it was unfair of her to leave
getting the breakfast to Uncle Charlie, especially when
she had had a day off yesterday, but her mind was a
mess of emotions and even a few minutes in which to
try and sort out her thoughts was too precious to lose.

Ever since she had come to bed last night she had
been trying to work out just what made James Arbory
tick. But last night her emotions had been too coloured
by the memory of the way he had made love to her,
skilfully arousing her passions until she had been
unable to deny him anything he had wanted. But, although she had gone farther with him last night than
any man before, he had stopped short of taking her
completely, had drawn back before things got out of
control and had left her feeling empty and frustrated,
her body aching for fulfilment. And that, too, was
something that she had worried and puzzled over until
the early hours when sleep had finally overcome her.

Now she tried to marshal her thoughts into some sort
of order and decided that the most disturbing problem
was why, when he already had a mistress, was James
Arbory also trying to seduce her. No, *had* seduced her,
as near as damn it, because last night she had *wanted*
him to take her and would willingly have given him her
virginity. She put her hands on her breasts beneath the
bedclothes, remembering how he had kissed and
caressed them, and her body trembled with agonised

longing. Then she turned convulsively and gripped her pillow hard, forcing her mind away from ecstasy and back to being objective. Was he just amusing himself? Was he the type of man who had to try his luck with every reasonably pretty girl who came his way, and once the seduction had been successful would drop her when he grew tired or when the next girl came along? But in that case where did Cynthia Marsden fit in? Perhaps, Pandora thought with bitter cynicism, he also liked to have a permanent mistress, an experienced woman who could cater to his more erotic whims as a young girl like herself could never do. She remembered someone saying that the last maid hadn't stayed long; had she, too, fallen a victim to Sir James' powers of seduction and then been cast aside? He had certainly gone from his mistress to her last night, she remembered.

But if all that were true, why then had he held back, and been so gentle with her when he had said goodnight? Did he, perhaps, intend to get rid of Cynthia Marsden and make her his mistress instead?

Pandora's mind ranged back and forth, finding many discreditable reasons for his treatment of her, but having every theory blown apart by the simple fact that he hadn't taken her when he could have done. In the end she sat up in bed and balled her hands into fists which she beat against her head. It was no use, she didn't know what to think, and she was only getting more and more confused. Only time would tell—that or some decisive action of her own to leave Arbory. But Pandora knew she couldn't do that; she was held here in his power as surely as a fly caught in a web who knows that the spider will eventually come for him.

That morning she went about her duties lethargically,

often pausing to stand staring into space, her thoughts far away, but at the same time her nerves were on edge in case James came near, but he was making his rounds of the farms on the estate today and wasn't expected back until the afternoon. During the morning Jon Thursby phoned to ask her to go out with him again, but she made an excuse, feeling quite unable to cope at the moment with his obvious wish for them to be more friendly.

'I haven't upset you or anything, have I, Pandora?' he asked anxiously.

'No. No, of course not. It's just that I'm not sure when I'll be able to get a day off now that the preparations for the Rose Ball have started,' she told him. Which, in a way, was true, because Uncle Charlie was making out lists of things to be done and was already contacting caterers and domestic agencies for extra staff.

After lunch, Pandora decided to take a walk to try to shake off her restlessness; at least it might help to stop her mind going round in circles all the time. The stables, of course, were out; Tom Langley had definitely put paid to any more walks in that direction and in so doing had lost her the solace she might have found there, so she turned her steps towards the lake and the summerhouse at the head of it. This had been built in the eighteenth century for the ladies of the house who would come here for picnics with their children or to read and draw. Several sketches by one more talented baroness had been framed and hung in the small room off the entrance hall where the tenants were shown to wait when they came to the house on estate business or to pay their annual rent in the days before telephones and banker's orders.

She walked slowly along the wide gravel path that ran round the edge of the lake, her head bowed in thought, hardly noticing the flowering shrubs or the sunlight reflected off the water, but when she reached the summerhouse she paused for a moment on the steps to look back at the house, her thoughts, though, still on its master. Then she shrugged her shoulders angrily and pushed the doors open to go and sit in the cool, shady interior. She was being an utter fool, she knew that. Always, since she had left school, she had prided herself on being sensible where boys were concerned, and not let herself get carried away by emotion or even curiosity, but now . . .! Now she was behaving like a cheap little idiot. Why, she had hardly known the man more than a few weeks and already she had let him—but it was much better not to think of that. Pandora dug her nails into her palms and tried to concentrate. What was it about him that made all her defences just melt away? He was handsome, yes, but she had been out with other good-looking men and they had never had this effect on her. She thought for a few minutes, picturing Sir James in her mind, and came to the conclusion that it was his arrant masculinity, his complete self-assurance that so overwhelmed her. That, and his sexual expertise. She had never met a man like him before and somehow was sure that she never would again.

Leaning back against the white-painted wall, Pandora sat in the sunlight of the open doorway, feeling warm and drowsy, the silence of the afternoon broken only by bird song and the far-off drone of a combine harvester reaping the first of the summer crop. Then she heard hasty footsteps outside on the gravel and her heart gave a crazy kind of lurch as a tall figure appeared suddenly in the doorway, blocking out the sun.

Pandora blinked, unable for the moment to focus, then stood up hurriedly when she realised that it was Tom Langley.

He crossed the floor and stood glaring at her, his face red and angry. 'I didn't think you'd dare to come to the stables again after last night, so I kept a lookout from the shrubbery and followed you round here. Why didn't you come when I called you? I told you it was all right.'

Pandora laughed shortly. 'You didn't really expect me to believe that, did you, after the way you behaved?'

'What do you mean, after the way I behaved? It was you who led me on, you little slut!' he retorted angrily. 'You girls are all the same, you let a chap spend his money on you and then get all prim and proper when they want a kiss or two in return.'

Coldly, Pandora said, 'It was you who kept on at me to go out, remember? And it was hardly my fault that you turned nasty when you couldn't get what you wanted.'

An angry flush of colour suffused his face and he took a step towards her.

'You keep away from me!' Pandora exclaimed. 'If you try anything again I'll scream the place down!'

'Huh, I wouldn't want to even touch you again now. I don't want Jon Thursby's leavings,' he said jeeringly. 'He's welcome to you for all I care.'

'Then get out of here and leave me alone.'

'Not till I get what I came for. Have you said anything about last night to anyone? *Have you?*' he repeated, catching hold of her wrist when she didn't answer at once.

'If you mean have I told anyone that you acted like a depraved animal, the answer's no,' Pandora retorted, then gave a cry of pain as he viciously twisted her wrist. 'You pig! Let me go!'

'Not until I'm good and ready.' He twisted her wrist again, smiling cruelly as he did so. 'There are other things you can do to a girl besides what I wanted to do to you last night, and if you dare to tell anyone about it then I'll have to . . .'

He broke off suddenly and made a strange gurgling sound in his throat, his hand letting go of her wrist as he was suddenly yanked off his feet.

'To do what? Just what was it you were going to do to Dora if she didn't keep her mouth shut?' James Arbory tightened his hold on Tom's collar and for all his size shook him by it like a dog. Tom yelped and tried to pull himself free but couldn't, his face becoming even redder than it had been before as his collar started to strangle him.

James looked at her. 'I take it this was the man you went out with last night?'

She nodded dumbly and his eyes lit with anger. 'I seem to remember warning you not to lie to me.' Pandora could only look at him helplessly until he said curtly, 'Get out. I'll speak to you after I've dealt with this young thug.'

There was a dangerous glint in his eyes, a look that she remembered seeing when he had accosted her on her motorbike, and she looked nervously from him to Tom, who was tearing at his shirt to try to open the collar. Involuntarily she said, 'Oh, please, don't hurt him.'

His face hardened, his mouth setting into a thin line. 'Get out!' he ordered again, his voice cold as ice.

She looked at him pleadingly, her green eyes anxious. 'But—his parents!'

His eyes came swiftly back to her, a different look in them this time, and he said more gently but no less compellingly, 'Go back to the house, Dora.'

For a moment longer she hesitated, then, knowing that any further attempt at intervention was useless, turned and ran out of the summerhouse and back towards the house, not stopping until she was out of breath and most definitely out of earshot. She wasn't sure what James had in mind for Tom Langley, but by the way he was holding him as if he didn't much care whether he strangled him or not, she was afraid Tom was in for a lesson he wouldn't forget in a hurry. And serve him right. But she couldn't help but be worried about the effect it would have on his parents. And James had said that he would speak to her after; that, too, wasn't something she was looking forward to at all.

But, although she waited in acute apprehension for a summons, James didn't send for her at all that day, and the next morning one of the cleaning women told them that Tom Langley was leaving Abbot's Arbory.

'Yes,' the woman passed on the gossip with great relish, 'seems he came home yesterday with a nasty black eye and bruises in other places I can't mention. At first his mother thought he'd been in a fight or something, but he said one of the horses had shied sudden when he was grooming it and it had knocked him down against a post. Then he comes out and says that he's been thinking of trying to get a job in a racing stables and that Sir James had agreed to give him a letter to take to a friend of his who trains horses at Newmarket. Ever so peculiar, isn't it? His ma said he hadn't mentioned to her about getting a new job, but then stands to reason he wouldn't tell her, would he? Because she's bound to try and stop him, Tom being her only one. But then his dad went to see Sir James and came back happy enough about it; said the boy ought to spread his wings a bit, so it's all settled and

Tom's going on Friday. There's one or two girls in the
village who'll be crying their eyes out this week, I can
tell you,' the woman added to Pandora in a lowered
voice so that Uncle Charlie couldn't hear. 'Several of
them had their eye on Tom at one time or another.'

Pandora listened with mixed feelings; feeling in-
expressibly relieved that Tom was going, and hoping
against hope that his parents didn't know the truth and
were blaming her for it. But Mrs Langley herself popped
into the kitchen the next day to use the washing machine as
hers had broken down, and it was evident from her conversation that she was completely in the dark, so Pandora was
able to feel that at least half her fears were allayed.

It seemed that James had forgotten his threat, for he
didn't send for her, and in fact she didn't see him at all
for the next few days as plans went ahead for the Rose
Ball and Uncle Charlie kept finding her extra jobs to do
connected with it, so that some of her usual work had
to be done later than normal. At first she had been nervous and tense as she waited for James' summons, but
when none came she felt a little piqued and instead of
being ready to hurry away if she heard him coming,
now she lingered longer than necessary about her jobs,
half hoping that he would walk into the room while she
was there. But when next she did see him it was quite
unintentional; because she had been helping to go
through the extra linen they would need for the guests
who would be staying the night after the ball, she had
almost forgotten to take fresh towels up to the master
bedroom, and she hastily picked up the pile and ran
upstairs with it before he went up to change for dinner.

But James must have come up earlier than usual, for
when she hurried into the room without bothering to
knock, he was already there, taking off the jacket of the

suit he had been wearing to attend a business conference in Oxford.

Pandora stopped short on the threshold. 'Oh! I—I'm sorry, I didn't think you'd be here. I've just brought up the clean towels.' Quickly she crossed to the bathroom and hung them on the rail.

As she emerged into the bedroom again she carefully kept her eyes averted and walked hurriedly to the door, but even as she reached to open it James said softly, 'Dora,' and she stood still, quivering, her hand gripping the knob hard.

'Come here.'

Slowly she turned to face him, her pulses racing. He was watching her enigmatically, his dark eyes narrowed, and instinctively she said, 'No.'

His mouth tightened for a moment, then he thrust forward his wrists and said coolly, 'Undo these for me, would you?' indicating the cufflinks set into his sleeves.

Still half afraid, Pandora moved hesitantly towards him and gave him a quick glance, but his face was quite impassive as he looked down at her, his expression unreadable.

As she began to undo the first link he said abruptly, 'I suppose you've heard that Tom Langley is leaving the stables?'

Pandora nodded without looking at him. 'Yes, I heard it from one of the cleaning women.'

'Why didn't you tell me it was him, Dora? Why did you lie and say it was someone from Oxford?'

She hesitated for only a second, but his free hand came up and clasped her arm fiercely.

'Answer me! Why did you lie?'

'Because—because I didn't want to get him into trouble.'

'You're so loyal, then? To a man who tried to rape you?'

His voice sneering, James added, 'If you care that much for him I wonder you didn't let him have what he wanted.'

Angry colour came into her cheeks. 'That isn't so at all! I couldn't care less what happens to Tom, but I like his parents very much and I didn't want them to be worried and upset. It was for their sake that I didn't tell you the truth.'

'You swear it?'

'Yes.' She glared up at him, still hurt and angry. 'Not that it's anything to do with you who I . . .'

But he interrupted her brusquely, 'Then why go out with him in the first place if you didn't like him?'

'I didn't want to, but he kept going on at me to all the time. And—and he accused me of being a snob.'

'I see.' He let go of her and she went on with her task. 'You should have trusted your instincts, Dora, and gone on refusing to go out with him. He's the type who gets dangerous when he's thwarted.'

She took out the first cufflink and looked down at it unseeingly. Speaking with difficulty, she said, 'And you? Should I trust my instincts where you're concerned, too?'

He smiled mockingly. 'Of course.'

Very carefully she took out the second cufflink and laid them both on the nearby dresser. With beating heart she said as steadily as she could, 'Then I'd better give in my notice and leave at once.'

'Perhaps that would be better.' Her eyes rose swiftly to his face at that and the mocking smile deepened. 'But you won't,' he went on softly. 'Because you've never experienced anything like this before. With me you're discovering a sexual awareness that you were too immature to know even existed. You're attracted to me, Dora, and there's no way you can leave here until I choose to let you go.'

Pandora stared at him in shocked horror, then turned to run away, but he swiftly caught her wrists, holding her prisoner. She made a convulsive movement to get free, but he was far too strong for her.

His eyes darkening, James said brusquely, 'Stop fighting me. You know you want it.'

'No!'

For a moment he was silent and then, to her surprise, he laughed mockingly. 'Oh, Dora, when *are* you going to stop saying no when you mean yes?'

'I don't! I—I . . .' Her voice faded and she stopped trying to break free. She gazed up at him, her mouth parting in a little sob of surrender, her eyes wide and dark in her pale face. 'Yes, oh, yes, James! *Please!*'

The next second she was pulled into his arms and his mouth was on hers, kissing her with a fierce hunger, a kiss that Pandora returned with passionate abandonment, uncaring about anything but the aching need that only he could assuage.

It was James who drew away first, again gripping her wrists as he put her from him, his fingers bruising her flesh, but for a different reason now. His eyes glittered down at her, his breathing uneven. His voice thick, unsteady, he said harshly, 'Help me undress.'

Pandora stared into his face for a long moment, then very, very slowly she lifted her hands and began to undo the buttons of his shirt. She reached the last one and hesitated again before opening the shirt and pushing it off his shoulders. He slipped his arms out of the sleeves and tossed it on the bed. He waited then, watching her, and his breathing quickened as she gently lifted her hands and very lightly, with just her fingertips, ran them along the broad width of his shoulders and on down to the hard, firm muscles of his arms. She touched them wonderingly, marvelling at his strength, her hands opening wide to take in their expanse. For a while she lingered there, but then her hands went back to his shoulders and this time moved slowly down the smooth, taut planes of his chest. He quivered, and then made a groaning sound deep in his throat as her fingers found, touched, explored, then trembled convulsively as he guided her head down and her lips, too, began tentatively to kiss and caress.

Suddenly he seized her arms and jerked her roughly against him, his hand coming up to wind itself in her hair as his mouth found hers with savage passion, his lips cruel and bruising.

'Dora! Oh, Dora, I want you. I want to take you, love you! I . . .' He broke off suddenly and then swore. 'Hell and damnation!' Then Pandora heard it too, the strident sound of the phone ringing persistently by his bed. His hands gripped her again and she could hear his heart hammering in his chest. He took a deep breath to try and control himself, then said imperatively, 'Wait! Don't go.'

Crossing to the phone, he picked it up and spoke while Pandora turned away, trying to stop herself from trembling and to collect her scattered wits. She crossed to the dresser and gripped its edge hard, lifting her head to stare at her reflection in the mirror. Her eyes were wide and uncertain, but there was a brilliant light in their green depths, so that her skin looked pale and translucent in comparison, and her lips, the lower one still trembling, were deep red from his assault on her mouth.

She heard James' voice rise in some annoyance. Then he said curtly, 'Very well, I'll be there about ninethirty,' and rang off.

He came up behind her, putting his hands on her shoulders. Their eyes met in the mirror and for a long

moment they gazed at each other, then James gently
turned her round and cupped her face in his hands. His
eyes warm, tender, he kissed her gently, then said
huskily, 'Darling, there's so much I want to say to you,
to tell you, but this is neither the time nor the place. I
have to go out on business tonight, but we'll talk tomorrow. Come to the library in the morning straight
after breakfast.' His lips touched her eyelids, the curve
of her cheek. 'Promise me you'll come.'

'Yes, all right.'

His mouth brushed hers lightly, but Pandora pushed
herself forward, clinging to his lips so that he had to kiss
her properly, and when at last they parted she opened her
eyes and gazed at him wonderingly. 'Oh, James!'

'Hush.' He put his finger to her lips. 'We'll talk tomorrow.'

She left him then and went to the kitchen to finish
preparing dinner, but she was in a kind of daze, doing
the cooking automatically and only mumbling a reply
when Uncle Charlie spoke to her. Luckily, however, he
was pretty preoccupied himself and didn't take too
much notice. But after he had served his master's meal
and they were eating their own, he made a sound as if
he was being poisoned and hastily pushed the strawberry mousse she had prepared away from him.

'Good God, girl, what on earth have you put in this?
It tastes terrible!'

'Does it?' Pandora had been gazing into space, but
now she looked down in surprise at her own plate.
Picking up her spoon she tasted it. A look of appalled
horror crossed her face. 'Oh, no! I put salt in it instead of
sugar.'

'*And* you gave the same dessert to Sir James,' her
uncle reminded her.

'Oh, lor! Didn't he say anything?'

He shook his head in puzzlement. 'No, he didn't. I wonder why that was? He certainly tasted it. But come to think of it he didn't eat much.'

'Perhaps he liked it?' she suggested hopefully.

Her uncle snorted derisively. 'No man in his right mind would like that!' And he got up to scrape his plate into the waste disposal and make a cup of coffee to get rid of the taste.

Pandora stared down at the mousse with a puzzled frown on her face. What on earth had made her do that? Anyone would think she was in love, or something equally . . . Her thoughts tailed off and she sat frozen. Was that the matter with her? Had she fallen in love with James Arbory? She shook her head, trying to clear it. It couldn't be so, it just couldn't! She stood up and abruptly pushed her chair away from the table. 'I think I'll go for a walk.'

Uncle Charlie stared after her in astonishment as she hurried out of the kitchen, but she just had to be alone for a while.

It was high summer now and not yet dark even though it was quite late in the evening. She ran down past the garage block and the high walls of the kitchen garden and into the open land at the side of the house, not stopping until she reached the first of the majestic oak trees that stood sentinel over the park. The evening sun was low on the horizon and lay like cloth of gold over the fields, casting long, deep shadows where the deer grazed slowly across the grass. Pandora leaned against a tree trunk and gazed back at the house, dazzled by the sun's reflection in a hundred window panes.

Perhaps that's what it is, she thought wildly. Perhaps I'm just dazzled by the house and by James' wealth. I can't be in love with him! It's just infatuation. To be in love with him would be all wrong, he stands for everything I despise! She tried to argue herself out of it, but the more she did so the stronger the feeling became. She began to walk agitatedly along the path, not caring where she was going. How could she possibly have fallen in love with someone whose whole way of life was such an anathema to her? It couldn't be love. It was just sex, that was all. The strongest sexual and physical attraction she had ever experienced. She stopped short suddenly, closing her eyes and trying to halt the chaotic thoughts in her mind, trying to let her feelings come through. And then, in that quietness, she knew, with blinding clarity, that she *was* in love with him. There would be no more doubts and questions ever again, and with that knowledge came the most wonderful sensation of happiness she had ever known. It seemed to bubble up inside her and burst out so that she spread her arms and whirled round and round, laughing aloud and wanting to shout and cry out with joy. It had never felt so good to be alive before. And to be young and in love was the most marvellous sensation that could ever happen to anyone. She ran through the park, startling the deer, leaping up to reach the leaves on the lower branches of the trees and throwing them up in the air, jumping over the shadows as her heart sang, 'I'm in love, I'm in love. I'm in love with James.'

She swung round to face the house again and sobered suddenly, face flushed, hair dishevelled. Like every other person since time began who has found themself in love, Pandora's first thought was whether James loved her in return. Her brow creased in anxiety. Their backgrounds, their principles, were so different. And she was only his maid! How could he possibly feel as she did? But then she remembered the way he had

looked at her earlier and his promise to talk to her tomorrow. Surely that could only mean that he, too, was
experiencing this most wonderful of all feelings?

It was almost ten o'clock and quite dark when
Pandora at last turned and began to make her way back
to the house. She went reluctantly, unwilling to have
this wonderful moment of discovery spoiled by the in-
trusion of ordinary everyday matters, but hoping that
she would be able to just say goodnight to Uncle
Charlie and go straight to bed, where she could lie and
think and dream, longing for tomorrow to come, but
half afraid of so much happiness.

A light shining through the open doors of one of the
garages helped to illuminate her way, but as she passed
the chauffeur, Travers, turned it off and closed the
garage doors.

He greeted her and fell into step beside her. 'I'm just
going up to the house to have a word with Mr
Richardson. Sir James gave me a message for him.'

'A message?' Pandora asked in surprise. 'Why can't
he give it to him himself? You have just brought him
back from wherever it was he went, haven't you?'

The man shook his head. 'No, I came back alone. I
took him to that Miss Marsden's.'

'Miss—Miss Marsden's?'

'Yes,' the chauffeur nodded, adding helpfully, 'She's
the one who lives on the other side of the village.'

'But you will be going to pick him up again later,
won't you?' Pandora asked tightly.

'No, he doesn't want me any more tonight.'

'But how will he get home?'

The man looked at her in some surprise and then
laughed scornfully. 'Use your loaf, Dora. He won't *be*
coming back. He's gone there for the night. And not for
the first time either.'

CHAPTER SEVEN

IT was early the next morning when Pandora let herself out of the side door, her note for Uncle Charlie saying 'Have decided to take today off', propped up on the kitchen table. She wheeled the motorbike out of its hiding-place and along the back drive to the tradesmen's entrance, not starting it up until she was safely outside the gates. The day was fine and sunny, the best kind of English summer morning, the July heat bringing the countryside to life and adding lustre to an already perfect setting. But Pandora was oblivious to it all and, although she had gone there with the firm intention of enjoying everything she saw, found herself wandering around Oxford aimlessly until she ended up sitting on the bank of the river, gazing blindly down into the rippling water.

Some students from one of the mixed colleges came along some time in the afternoon and drew her into conversation. They had stayed on in Oxford to do some extra studies during the long vacation and were all going to a party that night. They took Pandora under their wing and she went along with it more or less willingly, glad to have some of her own contemporaries around her, people who didn't ask questions or make demands of her. She went with them for a beans-on-toast type meal in one of the girls' rooms, and then later to the party which was being thrown at a flat in the town.

The people there, nearly all under twenty-five, dressed and behaved exactly as they pleased; if they wanted to let their hair down in the way they danced, it was okay by everyone else; if they wanted to make love they disappeared into another room for a while, and if they wanted to drink they brought their own bottles and that was okay, too. The music was loud and the room was hot and crowded with people. It was the kind of party that was Pandora's scene and where she should have felt right at home—but as the night wore on she found herself hating every minute of it! She danced with whoever asked her and laughed and drank red wine, ignored several passes that were made at her, and wished with all her heart that she had never seen either Abbot's Arbory or its master.

She left at about two in the morning when the party was still going strong and looked to last the whole night. At first she had been determined to stay till the end, but had suddenly been unable to stand any more and had collected her crash helmet and quietly slipped away. Strangely she wasn't tired, even though she had hardly slept the night before, but the fast ride through the deserted country lanes failed to invigorate her as it normally would. It was just a journey that had to be undertaken from A to B, and no longer the thrill of speed and power that it had always been before.

When she reached Abbot's Arbory she opened the gate, which fortunately was still unlocked, and turned off the engine to free-wheel down the long slope towards the house. She was surprised to see that there were lights still burning, in the kitchen area as well as in the main part of the house, although it was now nearly three o'clock. Her bike and the helmet she put back in the same place, then walked to the side door and quietly let herself in, intending to go straight to her room.

She hadn't thought that she had made any noise, but as she went down the corridor her uncle suddenly opened the door to the kitchen.

'Pandora!'

She jumped and turned rather guiltily. Uncle Charlie was wearing striped pyjamas under a maroon dressing-gown and looked far from pleased to see her.

'Where on earth have you been till this time of night? Don't you know it's three o'clock in the morning?'

Rather unbelievingly, Pandora said, 'You weren't waiting up for me, were you?'

'Of course I was. Otherwise I'd have been in my bed hours ago.'

'But why? I left a note to tell you I . . .'

'I've been worried to death about you,' he interrupted her brusquely. 'Ever since I realised you'd taken that hellish machine of yours. At two o'clock I even phoned up the County Hospital to find out if you'd had an accident.'

'I'm sorry, Uncle Charlie. I went to a party and . . .'

'A party?' His already angry face went redder than ever. 'And I suppose it never occurred to you that I might be worried and to pick up a phone to tell me where you were and that you'd be late?'

Pandora looked at him in some distress and then shrugged rather helplessly. 'No. No, it didn't.'

Her uncle snorted with rage until Pandora said slowly, 'You see, I'm not used to having someone worry about me,' which made him look rather shamefaced and turn away.

'Well, I wasn't the only one who was worried this time,' he told her, crossing to the house phone. 'Sir James came down here looking for you this morning and when I told him you'd taken a day off he said he wanted to see you as soon as you got in. Then when it got to eleven tonight he rang down and said I was to let him know when you got in, however late it was.'

He reached for the receiver and Pandora involuntarily put out a hand to stop him. 'Do you have to tell him?'

'Of course I have to tell him,' he answered testily. 'He ordered me to.'

'But, Uncle Charlie, I *have* to talk to you before I see him,' she said imploringly.

Her uncle looked at her anxious face, then sighed wearily. 'I don't for a minute suppose he'll want to see you at this hour. And *I* certainly don't want to talk.' He pressed the button for James' study and it must have been answered immediately, for he said almost at once, 'Yes, sir, she's just come in. Yes, quite all right. I gather she's been to a party.' He listened for a few seconds. 'I don't think that would be a very good idea, sir. Perhaps tomorrow. Very good, sir, I'll tell her.'

He put down the receiver. 'You're to see Sir James in his study at ten tomorrow.' He held up a hand as Pandora opened her mouth. 'And now I don't want to hear another word. I'm going to bed and anything you want to say to me will have to wait until morning.' He yawned and said, 'I'm not used to late hours.'

Pandora went to him and gave him a hug. 'I only wanted to say thank you, for waiting up—and for worrying,' she said huskily, then hurriedly turned and ran out of the kitchen and to her room.

The next morning found them both up on time, but neither of them looked very bright-eyed and bushy-tailed. Uncle Charlie was inclined to be short-tempered while Pandora had dark shadows around her eyes that told of another sleepless night.

She waited until her uncle had taken Sir James his morning coffee and then said firmly, 'Uncle Charlie, I have to talk to you. I'm going to relieve you of your biggest worry. I've decided to leave here.'

He looked at her, then poured out two mugs of coffee and put them on the table, motioning her to sit opposite him. 'Why?' he demanded bluntly.

She shrugged. 'I'm bored here. I think I'll go back to London. Today.'

'Where will you live till September? When you came here you said you had nowhere to go.'

Pandora looked down at her cup. 'I'll find somewhere.'

He looked at her searchingly. 'That's your only reason for wanting to go? You're sure?' His voice altered suddenly. 'You haven't broken something valuable, have you? That isn't why Sir James wants to see you?'

'No, it's nothing like that,' Pandora hastened to assure him. 'I told you—I'm just bored here in the country,' she lied, looking away.

He stared at her for a moment, then suddenly got to his feet. 'Well, I think you're being extremely selfish,' he said angrily. 'I've had to more or less deceive my employer so that you could have this job, and now you're throwing it back in my face. You *know* how hard it is to get a maid and yet you want to walk out this minute. *And* just as the Rose Ball is coming up and we're at our busiest. I think you're both selfish and ungrateful!'

Pandora gazed at him in consternation, completely

thrown by his attitude. 'But, Uncle Charlie, you don't understand.'

'Yes, I do. It suited you to come here, but now you've changed your mind. Met someone at this party last night and want to go off with them, for all I know. You young people are all the same,' he added indignantly, 'you have no thought or consideration for other people. But I must admit I'd thought better of you, Pandora!'

Biting her lip, Pandora sat in miserable silence; she had fully intended to leave this morning and never see James Arbory again, to run away from this first, disastrous love, and try and put it behind her, but she saw now that that was impossible unless she told Uncle Charlie the truth. She looked at his back as he huffily busied himself at the sink and knew that, much as she loved her only relative, she could never confide in him because he simply wouldn't understand, which meant that she had to either antagonise him, perhaps for ever, or stay. She stared into her coffee cup, longing to take the easy way out, but knowing that she was too soft-hearted to do it.

At length she said hollowly, 'All right, I'll stay until the ball.'

A decision which mollified her uncle but left Pandora to face her interview with Sir James. As ten o'clock came near she went to her room to tidy herself, pulling her hair back into a severe plait and making sure that her uniform skirt and blouse were clean and pressed. She delayed coming out of her room until the very last second and walked slowly through to the main part of the house, her heart beating loudly, and fighting an almost irresistible urge to turn and run. At the study door she halted as she tried to still her heartbeats, gritting her teeth in an effort to control herself. For a few moments she closed her eyes, willing herself to remember that he had gone straight from her to his mistress. And that helped—it helped considerably. Pandora's face was pale and tense, but her emotions were under control as she raised her hand and knocked on the door.

'Come in.'

James was sitting at a big mahogany desk set under the window, a working desk with neat piles of letters and files on its polished surface. He sat back in his chair as she came in, his grey eyes on her face. Carefully Pandora shut the door and turned to face him, but she kept her eyes fixed on a point above his head.

'You sent for me, Sir James,' she said tonelessly.

James stared at her for a few seconds, then threw a pen he was holding down on to the desk and stood up. 'Yes, I sent for you,' he agreed harshly. He came round the desk and strode towards her as she still stood by the door. A pulse began to beat in her throat, a sure sign that her nerves were at screaming point, but somehow Pandora stood her ground. 'You may recall that you made a promise to come here yesterday. A promise you didn't keep.'

He waited for her to speak, but Pandora continued to stare silently out of the window. Exasperatedly James put his hands on her shoulders and swung her round to face him. 'Why did you do it, Dora? Why just suddenly take off like that?'

Carefully avoiding looking at him, Pandora deliberately misunderstood. 'I hadn't had a day off for two weeks. I'm entitled to . . .'

'That isn't what I meant and you know it,' he interrupted fiercely, his eyes blazing with anger. His fingers

tightened on her shoulders and for a minute Pandora
thought that he was going to shake her, but then he
seemed to take a hold on himself because his grip loos-
ened and he sighed and said, 'Are you afraid of me? Is
that what it is?' His hand moved up to her face and he
began to trace the outline of her features with his
fingertips. Pandora's heart lurched and she had to dig
her nails into her palms to stop herself from shaking,
but still she didn't speak.

'You don't have to be afraid,' he said softly, insinuat-
ingly. 'Don't you know that you can trust me, that I'll
never do anything to hurt you?'

Her eyes flew bleakly to meet his and she shook with
inner rage; hadn't he already hurt her more than she'd
ever been hurt before?

He must have felt the tremor that ran through her
and mistaken it for desire, because he bent his head to
brush her lips with his. 'Oh, Dora, my darling, I . . .'

Pandora jerked her head away and stepped back.
'Will that be all, Sir James?' she demanded flatly.

For a moment he could only stare at her incredulously, then he said fiercely, 'No, damn it, that will *not*
be all! Why are you behaving like this? What's happened to make you change so suddenly?'

Again he waited for her to speak, but she just stood
there woodenly, her mouth stubbornly closed, her face
set.

'For God's sake, Dora, answer me!' He went to reach
out and catch hold of her again, but saw the sudden
flash of contemptuous anger in her green eyes and
stopped short. He stared at her, then said urgently,
'Dora, what is it? You *must* tell me.' Adding rather bit-
terly when she wouldn't answer, 'Does what was between us mean so little to you, then?'

Pandora slowly turned her head to look at him, realising that he had handed her a weapon with which to wound his inflated egotism. She shrugged disdainfully. 'A few kisses? Why should they mean anything?'

His eyes narrowed. 'They seemed to mean something to you at the time.'

She sniffed disparagingly. 'This is the twentieth century; petting sessions mean nothing to girls nowadays, not when they've been the whole way so often.'

A muscle jerked at his jawline and he flinched as though she had struck him a physical blow, and then a look of such murderous rage came into his eyes that for a moment Pandora's courage failed her, but she managed to add insultingly, 'And older men get so boring after a while. They always take themselves so seriously.'

His face tightened, went white, and if Pandora hadn't known that it was only his vanity that had been hurt, his manhood denigrated, she would almost have thought that it was pain that darkened his eyes and made him turn abruptly away and stand staring out of the window, shoulders hunched, his hands balled into fists in his pockets.

It was some minutes before he turned towards her again, and it seemed suddenly as if she was face to face with a stranger. His features were set into a stony mask, his eyes giving away nothing of what he was feeling. Only his voice betrayed him a little as he said harshly, 'I'm sorry you found my—attentions so boring, Dora. I gather you preferred those of the young men at the party you went to last night?'

'Yes,' Pandora lied boldly, desperately wishing that he would put an end to it.

'Well, you needn't worry, I shan't be bothering you again.'

She looked up then, surprised by his tone of voice, and for a brief second saw the mask slip as a look of bitter defeat came into his eyes. Then it was gone as he said icily, 'Very well, you can go back to your duties—and tell Richardson that I'm going in to Oxford and won't be in to lunch or dinner.'

Pandora obeyed him rather blindly, remembering that Cynthia Marsden had an antique shop in Oxford. So he was running back to her for solace already, for balm for his bruised ego, she supposed—and then cursed herself for a stupid fool as she felt bitter tears running down her cheeks. Fiercely she told herself that she had been right to do what she had, that he deserved nothing better, but then the racking, hollow pain of loss filled her heart and she wanted to turn and run back and tell him that it was all a lie and that she'd do anything he wanted, anything, so long as they weren't apart any more. And share him with another woman? Would she be willing to do that, too? Pandora's steps had automatically taken her to the library and she curled up at one end of the chesterfield, biting her knuckles as she tried to control herself. She had read of women, lots of them, who had loved a man so much that they were willing to sink their pride and tolerate another woman—or women—in his life, live for the few scraps of affection he was willing to show them from time to time.

But Pandora found that no way could she accept it. Okay, a love affair with him might not last for very long, perhaps only for a few months or weeks until James got tired of her, but in that time she would have to know that she was the only one, could never give herself with all the uninhibited passion of which she was capable if she knew there was someone else. She sat there for a long time, wishing desperately that she had someone to turn to for advice, to confide in, but there had been no one, not since her mother had died, and she suddenly felt as lonely now as she had done in those first terrible months of grief when there had only been Uncle Charlie, who had never had to cope with a child before, and had rather thankfully packed her off to boarding school because he thought he was doing the best thing for her. But somehow that memory helped; she had had to learn to live with loss then and she would do it now. She would be sure to always keep out of James' way, and although she owed it to her uncle to stay while he needed her, the moment the ball was over she would leave and find a job somewhere else for the rest of the summer.

If Uncle Charlie was curious about her interview with their employer, he took one look at her set face and refrained from questioning her, probably guessing that she had been told off for staying out so late. A lifetime of serving other people had made Uncle Charlie nothing if not tactful. He immediately gave her a job to do and kept her busy all day long, for which Pandora was profoundly grateful; the last thing she wanted right now was time to think.

But even though she had lots to do, the next two weeks to the ball dragged interminably. She managed to keep out of James' way, in fact he seemed to be out a great deal, but even so the house was full of his presence; it was impossible to go into a room without seeing some personal possession of his and she found it almost unbearable to go into his bedroom or the drawing-room with all the memories they evoked. Even her beloved library she entered with reluctance, because it was here that he had first kissed her.

Inevitably her unhappiness showed; she grew quiet

and withdrawn, her gay laughter no longer ringing round the kitchen to brighten up the dullest day. Although she continued to cook appetising meals for Sir James and her uncle, she only toyed with her own food, and this, together with throwing herself into cleaning the house and preparing it for its great day, made her lose weight and to look tired and drawn. At first her uncle had been convinced that she was just indulging in a fit of sulks because he hadn't let her leave when she wanted to, and decided to ignore her behaviour, he had enough on his plate with all the preparations without having to worry about a sullen niece. But after a few days even he began to realise that there was something wrong and clumsily tried to ask her what was the matter.

Pandora looked at him out of rather wistful, lost green eyes and shook her head. 'I'm fine, Uncle. Just rather tired, that's all.'

'Well, perhaps I have been working you a bit too hard. Why don't you take your day off tomorrow?'

She gave a small smile and looked away. 'There's too much to do.'

'We'll manage. You don't even go down to the stables for an hour or so any more. And Mr Thursby phoned up again for you yesterday, didn't he? Why don't you go out with him? You said you enjoyed it when you went before.'

'Yes, but I don't want to go again.'

'You haven't quarrelled with him, have you?'

Pandora gave a short laugh. 'Oh, no, Jon's too nice a person ever to quarrel with.' She stood up abruptly. 'There's just time to finish the job I was doing before I have to start getting dinner,' and she walked out of the kitchen with her uncle staring after her in bewilderment.

Now that Tom Langley had left there was nothing to
stop Pandora going down to the stables, but, as Uncle
Charlie had said, she never went there in the daytime in
case James might be there. She found it difficult to
sleep, often not dropping off until late or else waking in
the early hours and not being able to get to sleep again,
and sometimes then she would get up and dress in
sweater and jeans and go quietly out of the house and
down to the paddocks where the horses were out graz-
ing, or to the stable block to feed sugar lumps to
Greymist and the other mares in foal.

One night, only a couple of days before the ball, it
was particularly bad; she woke in her little room and
heard the soft patter of rain on the window, tried to go
to sleep again, but could only toss and turn and think,
think of nothing but James and everything she was
trying so hard to forget. At length, when the light
coming through the curtains grew stronger, she got up
and washed and dressed, brushing her hair but leaving it
hanging long and loose on her shoulders. She slipped on a
mac and filled the pockets with sugar-lumps, then let
herself out and ran down to the stableyard, unheedful of
the rain on her bare head, her hair flying out behind her.

The sky was grey overhead, but in the distance the
clouds were thinner with just a touch of blueness in
their depths, giving the promise of dryer weather and
sunshine later in the day.

Greymist came as soon as she had opened the top
half of her door and Pandora spoke to her lovingly.
'Hello, my beauty, how are you today? It's your kind of
day this morning.' She stayed talking to the mare for
about ten minutes before moving on and then stood at
the arched entrance looking out over the park to the
mist-hung hills beyond. A frustrated restlessness filled

her, adding to her unhappiness; she longed for some-thing, anything to happen, what she didn't know. Suddenly she turned and ran to the tack room where she took down a bridle and exercise saddle, then went back to the stables to the stall of one of the new stal-lions that James had brought back from Ireland. He was a beautiful creature, a big three-year-old chestnut with a white blaze and powerful shoulders, who had won several races. Pandora talked to him, but he snorted a little and moved impatiently while she saddled him, eager to be off.

Leaving her mac in the stall, Pandora swung herself up and the horse started to move even before she had got her right foot in the stirrup.

'Hey, wait for me!' she laughed, and patted the horse, leading him out of the yard and down between the pad-docks towards the rain-shrouded hills. Once clear of the fences she let him break into a canter and set him at a fallen tree trunk, to find out if he had been a steeple-chaser. He cleared it with feet to spare and went over a stone wall dividing the park from the open ground beyond as if it was a kerb.

Pandora brushed rain from her face and bent low over the horse's neck. 'All right, boy, let's go!' And she kicked him into a fast gallop, thundering over the undulating countryside in a long, powerful stride as if he was once again competing in a race. Pandora laughed aloud, loving every minute of it, the rain on her face, the wind blowing her hair out behind her like a second mane, almost the same colour as that of the horse.

After a mile or so she turned the horse's head to make a gradual half circle and slowed down a little, her shoulder and thigh muscles aching after not having

ridden for years, realising that if she wanted to get the
horse back and groomed before the stables came to life
she ought to turn back now. She turned the horse towards Arbory, and then stiffened. Another rider was
coming fast towards her, cutting across from the stables
in a diagonal line that would bring him directly to her.
Pandora had no difficulty in recognising either rider or
horse. It was James Arbory on the big black hunter he
always rode.

Her heart gave a wild jolt that communicated itself to
the horse, because he plunged to one side suddenly,
almost unseating her. Blind panic at the thought of
having to face James again took over and she gave the
horse his head, steering him in the direction of a pine-
wood with the crazy idea that she might be able to lose
him there. She reached the trees first and dived through
the thick undergrowth of bracken that reached up to
her stirrup in places, bending low over the saddle to
avoid the branches that brushed against her. The wood
was very quiet, there was no noise except the startled
cries of birds who flew up into the air as she passed, the
heavy noise of the stallion's breathing, the thud of his
hooves on the soft ground, and the echoing sounds of
her pursuer coming up fast behind her.

Pandora pushed the stallion as hard as he would go;
he was probably much the faster horse of the two, but
he wasn't used to this soft, uneven ground and he had
already had one good gallop and was tiring, although
he gallantly pushed himself to his limit when she urged
him on. They weaved their way through the trees and
jumped a wide, fast-flowing stream as Pandora tried to
shake James off, but then she came unexpectedly on a
clearing where rain made whirlpools on the surface of a
large pond, and she had to swerve to avoid dashing into

it, breaking the horse's stride and slowing him down for
a few precious seconds.

It was all James needed. The next minute his horse
was alongside and his left hand reached out for her
bridle, pulling the stallion up so suddenly that the
animal reared and plunged and it took all Pandora's
skill to stay in the saddle.

She turned on him, eyes blazing. 'Let go of my bridle!
Damn you, how dare you . . .' Her words were cut off
abruptly as James put his arm round her waist and
lifted her bodily out of the saddle. For a moment she
was held firmly against him, but then he had scooped
her rein out of her hand so that he had both horses and
dropped her unceremoniously to the ground.

Pandora cried out as she landed, but it was her dignity that was hurt far more than her behind. She yelled
at James angrily, but he had dismounted himself and
was tying the reins to a tree. Then he turned and came
purposefully towards her.

Pandora took one look at his face, stopped yelling
and turned to run. He caught her before she had even
gone two yards and dragged her back.

'You crazy little fool! You could have killed yourself
in this wood!' He shook her violently, his hands gripping her arms. 'I ought to put you over my knee and
give you the hiding of your life!'

For a terrified moment Pandora thought that he was
going to carry out his threat and she started to struggle.

'Let me go! Damn you, let me go!' She raised her
hand to hit him, but he was too fast for her and caught
her wrist. Furiously she opened her mouth to yell at
him again, but was suddenly still. James was staring
down at her, his face set and tense, the anger still there
but subdued before a deeper emotion.

His fingers tightened, biting into her flesh. 'Why did you run away from me? Why?'

'I—I don't know.' The rain was falling heavier without the protection of the trees, wetting her hair and plastering it to her head. A drop trickled down her face. Almost absentmindedly James put up a thumb to brush it away, then put his hand on her neck as he studied her face.

In little more than a whisper, Pandora said shakily, 'Please don't—touch me.'

'Why not?'

She didn't answer—couldn't.

'What is it, Dora? Why have you changed towards me so suddenly?'

Her hands began to tremble and she turned her head away, biting her lip.

Immediately, roughly, he pulled her back. 'Don't turn away from me. Tell me, Dora. *Trust me.*'

He said it urgently, persuasively, but her eyes darkened as she stared into his face. How could she possibly trust him now? Lifting her arm, she knocked his hand away, her green eyes glaring defiance. 'I said don't touch me!'

It was the wrong thing to do. His face hardened and he grabbed her round the waist, pulling her against him and forcing her head back as his lips found hers. It was quite some time before he released her mouth and even then he didn't let her go, holding her head close against him so that she could hear the rapid beating of his heart in his chest.

'Is this the only way I'm going to get through to you?' he demanded raggedly. 'Won't you ever learn to trust me?'

'No!' She tried to pull away. 'You're just playing with

me. Just amusing yourself by trying to make me fall for you, but . . .'

'So that's it! I thought as much. Oh, Dora, if you only knew the half of . . .' He bit off what he was going to say and instead said urgently, 'Listen, I want you to do something for me. I want you to try and remember how you felt when I kissed you—now and before. Just your feelings, nothing else. We had something good going for us—I know you felt it too. Just think about it, Dora, and let your heart guide you, not all those stale prejudices you've had indoctrinated into you over the years. Promise me you'll try.'

Pandora stared at him, then looked away wretchedly. Did he really dare to ask so much of her? 'I don't know. I don't see any point.'

'But you'll try?'

Grey eyes gazed earnestly into green and she found herself capitulating against her will. She nodded. 'Yes, all right,' she agreed huskily.

'Good girl.' His eyes warm, he bent to kiss her again, but she deliberately turned her head away and after a moment he let her go, then turned and walked to the horses. 'Who taught you to ride?' he asked.

Pandora accepted the change of subject thankfully. 'My father. I was riding almost before I could walk.'

James raised his eyebrows as he brought the horses over and handed her the chestnut's rein. 'I thought you said you were an orphan. Or was that, too, part of your cockney charade?' he asked quizzically.

Pandora flushed. 'No. My father was killed when I was only eight.'

'He was killed?'

'Yes. He was in the R.A.F. Something went wrong with his plane and it crashed.'

'And your mother?'

'She died of cancer a few years later.'

Pandora thought she said it quite matter-of-factly, but James gave her a swift glance and covered her hand with his. 'I'm sorry.'

'Don't be.' Deliberately she moved her hand away. 'It was a long time ago and I'm quite capable of looking after myself now,' she told him with a defiant toss of her head.

'Of course,' James agreed smoothly. He looped his own rein over his arm and joined his hands together to make a step for her, hoisting her easily into the saddle. 'And didn't you mention a relative, an uncle or something?'

An imp of mischief came into her eyes and made her smile. 'Oh, yes, I have Uncle Charlie.'

James swung himself up into his saddle and came close up alongside her. 'Do that again, would you?'

Her eyebrows rose questioningly. 'What?'

'Smile.' He leaned forward and took her hand, carrying it to his lips. 'Because you so seldom smile for me, and because you look so very lovely when you do.'

But Pandora didn't smile, she could only stare at him as he bent to kiss her palm, then closed her fingers so that the kiss was like a tangible thing, held close in her hand.

They were mostly silent as they rode slowly back through the wood and down to the stables. The rain had stopped now and a weak sun was pushing aside the clouds to make the raindrops sparkle like diamonds on the leaves and the grass. The house, too, had a scrubbed clean look, the golden stone soaking up the sun and looking brand new, and yet as old as time itself. Unconsciously Pandora reined in as she gazed across at the house, never tiring of filling her eyes with its beauty.

James, too, stopped, but he was looking at her, not the house. In a rather strange tone he said, 'You've fallen in love with it, haven't you?'

She shot him a swift look and said lightly, 'How can you fall in love with a pile of stone and mortar?'

'Very easily. My family have been doing it since it was first built,' he told her with a rather wry twist to his mouth.

Curiously she asked, 'What does it feel like—to own all this? To be the master of Abbot's Arbory?'

He shrugged. 'Sometimes it feels like a millstone around my neck; when the harvest is bad and the roof leaks yet again. And it can be a lonely place when you have no one to share it with. But at other times, times like this, you realise that you've been granted a great privilege in being able to live in it and take care of it until it's time to hand it on to the next generation—or to the nation if they keep up their iniquitous taxes or decide to nationalise the land as you'd like,' he added drily.

Pandora flushed, remembering that conversation in Oxford, but before she could speak, he went on, 'We'd better be getting back. You're soaking wet. Why did you come out without a jacket or a scarf?'

'I don't know—I didn't think about it. Anyway, I like the rain.'

When they reached the stables he took the horse from her. 'I'll see to him. You go back to the house and get into a hot bath.'

'Oh, but I ought to groom him and see that he's . . .'

'Dora,' he said in a tone that made her stop short, 'do as you're told.'

Her eyes lit with amusement. 'Yes, Sir James,' she agreed demurely.

She turned to go, but his voice stopped her. 'And Dora—remember what we agreed.'

Her face grew serious again, and she gazed at him for a long moment before nodding briefly and hurrying back to the house.

But there was little time to think over the next two days as the house seemed to be invaded by an army of outside caterers, florists and musicians. And impossible to dissociate herself from the air of excitement and bustle that seemed to fill Uncle Charlie and everyone else as the time for the ball drew near. The house shone inside as well as out, every room cleaned and polished, the ballroom and all the reception and guest bedrooms filled with flowers, the doors open and welcoming.

Sir James' aunt, Lady Townley, arrived the day before and went over the house with Uncle Charlie following anxiously at her heels, but she had no fault to find and was unstinting in her praise, which pleased him immensely. She also chatted to Pandora when she brought her evening dress up after pressing the creases out.

'Such a pity you're only here for the summer, Dora. You seem to be settling in so nicely. When do you go back to college?'

'In September. But how did you . . .?'

Lady Townley raised her eyebrows. 'How did I know you were a student? James told me, of course. He's told me quite a lot about you. He does confide quite a few things to me, you know.'

Pandora had left then, but the remark had puzzled her. She couldn't understand why Lady Townley had said it, or why James had bothered to tell his aunt anything about herself. You would have thought he would have kept his sexual affairs from his relatives.

On the evening of the ball she dressed in her best uniform, expecting to take the women's wraps as they arrived, but James told Uncle Charlie that she was to stay in the kitchen quarters and that a hired maid could see to the coats. Pandora was first astonished, then angry. 'Did he say why?' she demanded.

He shook his head. 'Probably wants you to keep an eye on the caterers while I'm upstairs,' he remarked, too busy to be really bothered.

Pandora's face fell with disappointment. For what seemed like weeks she had been helping to prepare for this party, and now she wasn't even to see it. Not that it was her kind of scene, of course, but she had been looking forward to seeing the clothes the women wore and that kind of thing. But there was plenty to do in the kitchen and she had no time to be more than mildly resentful until after the buffet supper had been served, then she sneaked up the back stairs and round on to the main landing which ran round the entrance hall and where she could see several of the guests and hear the distant sound of the band. The big front doors were wide open and many people were going outside to stroll through the lantern-hung rose garden. As Pandora watched, a foursome, two women followed by two men, came back into the house and one of the women turned to catch hold of the arm of the man behind her, her laugh ringing out as she spoke to him. The other three were strangers, but Pandora would have recognised that laugh anywhere. It was Cynthia Marsden.

She stiffened with shock. Was that why James had ordered her to stay in the kitchens? Because he didn't want her to know his mistress was here? Or even vice

versa? For the first time it crossed her mind that
Cynthia Marsden might be suspicious of James' new
maid, might even have told him to get rid of her, so that
she, Pandora, was being kept out of the way to keep his
mistress sweet. Rage soon gave way to a need for re-
venge, and without stopping to think she ran to the
back stairs and down to her own room. She yanked off
her uniform, tearing it in her hurry, and with hands
which she had to force herself to steady she drew her
hair back and coiled it into a sophisticated style, then
made up her face with eyeshadow, highlights, blusher,
the whole works. The she crossed to the wardrobe and
took out The Dress, an haute couture creation that she
and three of her friends had, in a mad but never re-
gretted moment, clubbed together to buy from one of
those little shops in Chelsea that specialise in good
secondhand clothes that have been worn for a season or
until the original owners get tired of them. It was a
beautiful thing; in a burnt orange with diamanté straps
and a low back, but cut so well that its simple lines
clung and yet covered, revealing nothing and yet sug-
gesting everything. With Pandora's colouring it looked
superb, and she thanked her stars that it had been her
turn to use it for these holidays. She fished out the bag
that went with it and put on her only pair of decent
evening shoes, then for good measure splashed on the
last of the French perfume that she had been carefully
hoarding. If she was going to spoil James Arbory's
game she might as well go the whole hog!

Picking up her skirts, she hurried through the back
way to the main house again, waited for some
women to go down the staircase and fell in behind
them. Her heart was thudding with anger rather than
trepidation, but her face was serene as she walked,
head held high, into the ballroom.

It was only just midnight, people had finished supper and the dancing was beginning to be in full swing again. Pandora glanced round but couldn't see anyone she knew, so she began to walk round the room towards the other end. Almost at once a young man came up to her and said that he was sure they'd met somewhere. She let him get away with the lie and accepted his offer to dance; it was as good a way as any of looking round the room and finding out where James was.

They went slowly round the dance floor, the young man trying to arouse her interest, but Pandora looking round all the time and answering him abstractedly. He wasn't a very experienced dancer and twice they bumped into other couples. The second time the woman tutted with annoyance and Pandora turned her head to find herself only a foot away from Cynthia Marsden. The older girl looked at her for a moment with a slight frown, as if she was trying to place her, then gave a little nod and a half smile, the way you do when you recognise someone's face but can't remember where you met them. Pandora nodded demurely in return, hiding the imp of devilment in her eyes.

Shortly afterwards she saw James; he was talking to Lady Townley and an elderly couple near the entrance to the library, but as she got nearer he glanced up and let his eyes run over the dancers. His eyes fell on her and he stopped short in what he was saying, his eyes widening.

Pandora looked at him balefully. So he'd complained that she didn't smile at him enough, had he? Well, she'd soon remedy that! As she came opposite him, she opened her mouth and gave him her most dazzling smile, letting her whole face light up with it.

His left eyebrow rose and then he raised the glass in his hand in a silent toast, bowing his head in acknowledgment.

And *he* probably didn't even recognise me either, Pandora thought as her partner turned and she was hidden from his view. But I'll make sure they both do before the evening's over.

When the music stopped she resolutely refused to dance with the young man again and walked through into the room where the drinks were being served. A waiter gave her a glass of champagne and she carried it back into the ballroom, standing near one of the stone pillars where she could watch the dancers. Cynthia was dancing again, with a different man this time, and gave Pandora a long, puzzled look as she passed. Her glass empty, Pandora placed it on the tray of a passing waiter and exchanged it for another full one. She found that she rather liked this champagne, the only time she had ever tried it before was at the twenty-first birthday celebrations of a fellow student, and then it hadn't seemed to taste much different from cider, but this was quite different, a much nicer taste; in fact she had a feeling that she could quite get to like champagne, after all.

'Pandora?' Her name was said on a questioning note and she turned to see Jon Thursby standing nearby.

She smiled. 'Don't look so worried; it really is me. How are you?'

'Oh, fine. I wish I'd known you'd be here; I'd have asked you to dance earlier.'

'I didn't know I was going to be here myself until a few minutes ago.' Across the floor she saw James excuse himself from the people he had been with and look around the room. She drained her glass and looked round for somewhere to put it.

'I don't understand. How could you not know you were coming?' Jon asked with a frown. 'Didn't Sir James tell you until tonight, or something?'

'He didn't tell me at all,' Pandora replied baldly. 'I

suppose you could say that I'm a gate-crasher.' She saw that James was making his way round the room, politely exchanging a word with people who claimed his attention, but purposefully heading in her direction. Rather unsteadily she held out her glass to Jon. 'Look, do you think you could get me another one of these?'

'Yes, of course.' He looked round for a waiter, but there wasn't one near. 'I'll have to go to the bar. Shan't be more than a minute.'

Someone had caught hold of James' arm and was insisting on taking a drink with him, then the dance ended and everyone crowded off the floor, getting in the way so that she couldn't see him any more. Pandora looked away and found herself looking straight into Cynthia Marsden's cold blue eyes as she came to stand beside her.

'I thought as much!' the older girl exclaimed. 'You're the maid! What are you doing here?' Her eyes widened. 'Sir James didn't give you permission to come, did he?' she asked sharply.

Pandora's chin came up. 'No, he didn't.'

'Of all the nerve!' Cynthia's voice had risen slightly and one or two heads turned towards them.

She opened her mouth to say something else, but James suddenly appeared at her side and asked, 'Is something the matter, Cynthia?'

'Can't you see?' She indicated Pandora with a disdainful hand. 'Although I admit I had to look twice before I could believe my eyes. It's your new maid!'

'So it is,' James agreed softly, and Pandora raised reluctant eyes to meet his. The arrested expression she had seen once before—when she had run into the kitchen on that first morning with her arms full of flowers—was back on his face now, but there was also a bright flame in his eyes that sent sudden electric shock waves running through her, The atmosphere seemed to be charged with the current that ran between them, a current generated by two people who desperately want to make love but haven't been able to do anything about it.

The silence seemed to last for ever until Cynthia said fiercely, 'She's no right to be here. She's admitted that you didn't invite her.' And looked as if she would very much like to have ordered him to send Pandora away, if she had dared.

'No, but I did.'

With a physical effort Pandora tore her eyes from James and saw that Jon Thursby had come to stand beside her. He put a hand on her shoulder. 'Pandora is with me,' he said firmly.

James' head came up at that and his eyes narrowed.

Cynthia looked at Jon in amazement. 'With you? But you hardly know her, surely?'

'On the contrary. Pandora and I have met many times at the stables and we've dated before, so it was only natural that I should invite her to be my partner. Not,' he added roundly, 'that I think it's any concern of yours, Cynthia.'

The blonde girl looked taken aback and opened her mouth to make an angry retort, but James intervened smoothly, 'No, indeed. And I'm sure, Jon, that you won't mind lending your partner to me for this dance.' And he took hold of Pandora's hand and led her firmly on to the dance floor.

The music had just started and there were only one or two other couples on the floor. For a few seconds he looked down at her enigmatically, waiting for her to come to him. Slowly she moved into his arms, her eyes never leaving his face. Gently but compellingly he pulled her close against him. Slowly they began to move around the floor in time to the music, although what the tune was Pandora had no idea. Every nerve end seemed to be on fire and her hand began to shake. James closed his over it tightly, his clasp warm and strong, and held it against his chest. People turned to stare at them as they danced, wondering who she was, asking their neighbours, but Pandora was quite impervious, lost to everything but the awareness of his body hard against her own, the warmth of his hand and the fire deep in his eyes.

More people moved on to the floor, filling it, but she didn't notice them; they seemed to be alone, encased in a glass bubble, like an ornament on a Christmas tree, with everything around them just distant sounds and shadows. Then James broke the spell by letting her go. For a moment she was bewildered, unsure where she was, but he tucked her hand under his arm and led her out through the long doors that lay open to the garden. He walked her down through the rose garden where other couples were strolling under the lanterns and on into the darker paths between the box hedges to a part where a stone balustrade overhung the lake. It was very quiet, the sounds from the house muted, the night heavy with the scent of honeysuckle.

James put his hands on her waist. 'You're trembling,' he said softly. 'Are you cold—or just afraid of me?'

She shook her head dumbly, knowing that it was neither.

'You minx! Why didn't you tell me your name was Pandora?'

She lifted her hands and rested them on his shoulders. 'I don't know. I felt that I—I had to hold something of myself back from you. That I couldn't just give you—everything.'

His hands tightened on her waist. 'But you told Jon Thursby. You were willing to confide in him,' he added on a harsher note.

'And what if I did?' Pandora retorted, immediately on the defensive. 'He was very kind to me.'

'Was he, by God!'

'Yes, he was. Which was more than you ever were,' she exclaimed hotly.

'No,' he agreed drily. 'That wasn't how you made me feel. I needed to arouse stronger emotions in you than kindness would ever have done.'

His words made her stop short, trying to discover his meaning, but it was too much to cope with and she pushed it aside. 'Why did you order me to stay in the kitchen tonight?' she demanded.

His mouth twisted a little, whether in mockery or amusement, she couldn't tell. He didn't answer her question, instead drawing her closer against him and saying, 'Did you know your eyes change colour when you're angry? Go from ice green to fiery emerald?'

'What's that got to do with it?' Pandora exclaimed indignantly.

'Everything,' he answered calmly. 'It was what first made me realise how much I loved you.' Then he smiled at her astonished face and bent his head to kiss her.

When James at last lifted his head, he held her trembling body close in his arms and said jerkily, 'Darling, earlier you said that you felt as if you had to hold back from me. Do you still feel like that?'

'No! Oh, no.' She reached up and touched his face wonderingly. 'I love you. I love you so much it hurts.'

'Sweetheart!' His hand covered hers as he buried his

face in her palm. His voice muffled, he said, 'And you're happy now to give yourself to me?'

Her hand fluttered in his, but she replied unhesitatingly, 'Yes.'

'Oh, darling!' He pulled her roughly to him, holding her close. 'If you only knew how much I want you! It's like an ache deep inside me that's always there, and sometimes it gets so bad it almost drives me crazy. It was hell trying to ...' He broke off abruptly as the sound of voices, a man's cajoling, a girl giggling, reached their ears. They stood in silence for a while, hoping the intruders would go away, but it was evident that they, too, had slipped into the garden for a spot of lovemaking.

'We'd better go in,' James said softly. 'Lord, if only I wasn't the host and could just spirit you away tonight! There's so much I want to tell you, so many plans to make. But we'll have to wait until tomorrow, until we have Abbot's Arbory to ourselves again.'

He kissed her again and then put his arm possessively round her waist and led her back to the house.

CHAPTER EIGHT

THEY went back into the ballroon through the french
doors and almost immediately James was buttonholed
by one of the guests. Pandora hung back, but he kept a
tight hold of her arm and motioned with his free hand
to one of the waiters who brought them fresh glasses of
champagne. For the second time that evening James
raised his glass in a silent toast to her, but how different
it was now from an hour ago. Then she had been angry
and vengeful, but now she would have felt intoxicated
even without the champagne. Her heart sang; she had
committed herself to him and it was wonderful. She had
told him she loved him, promised to give herself to him
whenever he wanted, and she didn't give a damn! Her
own moral scruples and her innate dislike of anything
sordid or scandalous were lost beneath the overwhelming passion she felt for James. How could love ever be
scandalous, how could the consummation of love ever
be sordid?

His conversation over, James quickly led her on to
the floor again before someone else could interrupt; but
to be held by him, to touch him and to feel his hands on
her was so tantalisingly exciting that Pandora could
hardly bear it. Almost she was glad when the band
swung into a faster number and he took her off the
floor.

Jon was nowhere to be seen, but almost as if she had
been waiting for them, Cynthia came up immediately
and said sharply, 'James, I'd like to speak to you.
Alone,' she added when James showed no sign of letting
go of Pandora's hand.

He frowned slightly, but turned to Pandora. 'Wait for me, I won't be long.'

But Pandora shook her head. 'No. I'd rather leave now and see you tomorrow.'

'Very well.' His hand tightened on hers for a moment and then he let her go, watching her as she went quickly out of the ballroom.

Many heads turned to look at her as she walked, tall and slender, her face radiantly happy, through the corridors towards the main hall, but Pandora was hardly aware of anyone else, she was still in a dazed, dreamlike state with her feet at least six inches off the ground. She paused in the hall, undecided whether to go out into the gardens again.

'Can I help you in any way, madam? A glass of champagne, perhaps?' asked a polished voice at her elbow.

Pandora turned and smiled. 'No, thank you, Uncle Charlie, I've a feeling I've had too many already.'

'Pandora!' He almost dropped his tray in surprise, then lowered his voice to a wailing hiss as he looked wildly around. 'Get back to the kitchens quickly! Oh, my God, I knew it was too good to be true!'

He shepherded her through the baize door to the kitchens and then turned to her angrily. 'Haven't you got any sense in your head? What on earth possessed you to do it? Did Sir James see you?' he asked anxiously.

Pandora smiled. 'Oh, yes, he saw me all right. In fact he danced with me.'

Her uncle groaned hollowly and sat down heavily in a chair. 'I knew it, I knew you'd get me the sack before you were through! I ought to have listened when you said you wanted to leave and let you go.'

Impulsively Pandora caught hold of his arms and pulled him to his feet, then swung him round. 'Forget about your silly old job, it's quite safe. Oh, Uncle Charlie, the most wonderful thing has happened! I've fallen in love! Really, really in love.'

He pulled himself free, his dignity seriously impaired, and looked at her with alarm. 'Who with?' he demanded apprehensively, then added more hopefully, 'Is it Jonathan Thursby?'

'No,' Pandora answered impatiently. 'With Sir James, of course.'

He made a strangled kind of noise and sat down again. 'But—but you can't be. It's impossible!' He tried to pull himself together. 'Pandora, you're just infatuated, that's all. You'll soon get over it.'

She went down on her knees and put her hands in his. 'No, Uncle Charlie,' she said softly. 'This is the real thing. I've fought against it almost since I first got here and I know I'm really serious.'

Something in her voice must have convinced him, because he didn't try to persuade her any more, but instead said, 'It's no good, child. You've got to leave here now and try and forget him. He'll never marry you—not someone who's been his maid.'

For a moment her eyes shadowed and she looked away. 'I know. I've always known that. But I'm not looking for marriage. I've never expected that.'

He stared at her. 'Do you mean to say that you're willing to—to live in sin with him?' he demanded, his face white with shock.

She nodded, and he exploded then, telling her not to throw her life away, that she'd always regret it, and much in the same vein, until Pandora cut sharply across his anger. 'It's no use arguing, Uncle Charlie. He's already asked me and I've agreed.'

He was silent, turning his back on her as he busied

himself in the kitchen. The internal phone rang and he crossed to answer it. 'You're wanted in the library,' he told her, his face still set and angry.

It could only be James. Pandora's feet flew as she went by the back way, avoiding the guests. She pushed open the door of the library, her face lighting up with expectation, but there was only Cynthia Marsden waiting for her, a triumphant sneer on her face.

'Come in and shut the door,' she commanded peremptorily.

Slowly Pandora obeyed, eyeing the older girl suspiciously.

'Sir James has asked me to speak to you—no, perhaps it would be more honest to say that I insisted on telling you myself.' She waited, but when Pandora didn't speak, went on, 'To tell you that any understanding you think you had with Sir James no longer stands. Let me explain,' she added when she saw the look of disbelief in Pandora's eyes. 'Sir James and I are very old—friends. He has asked me to marry him several times, but I have always refused because I value my independence and had no wish to be tied down by marriage. Sir James, however, became impatient and he decided to try to make me change my mind by making me jealous. Rather old-fashioned tactics, I must admit, but still effective. And he used you to do so.'

Pandora stared at her in horror. 'I don't believe you,' she burst out.

'No?' Cynthia smiled sneeringly. 'But you hardly thought he could be serious about a servant, surely? But his ruse did work; I did feel jealous, and I'll admit that tonight I really thought that he might be contemplating amusing himself by having an affair with you. Afterwards he assured me, of course, that he had only done it to provoke me, but one can never be completely sure where men are concerned, can one?'

'Afterwards?' Pandora asked in little more than a whisper.

'After I agreed to be his wife.'

Her brain almost paralysed with shock, Pandora said protestingly, 'But—but you can't be! He told me. He said he . . .'

'That he loved you? You surely didn't believe him?' The other girl crossed to the desk and took a cigarette from a silver box, lighting it with the desk lighter. She blew away the smoke and looked disdainfully at Pandora. 'You're really very naïve, aren't you? Exactly right for James' purpose. Surely you realised that he has a great deal of experience where women are concerned? In someone like you he can produce any reaction he wants. And telling you he loves you was guaranteed to lift you into this state of dewy-eyed idolatry so that I was bound to notice. Although I doubt if he could have borne to have you drooling over him and clinging to his hand like a lovesick puppy for very long.' She laughed mirthlessly. 'I shall have to remind him of what I've saved him from. But in the meantime,' she opened the top drawer in the desk and took out an envelope, 'he asked me to give you this. It's your wages, together with a bonus for the—er—services you unwittingly rendered. But now that you've served your purpose I want you out of the house at once. You can leave first thing to-morrow morning, and please don't try to see Sir James again, because you'll just be wasting your time.'

Pandora stared first at Cynthia and then at the envelope she held out to her. With a little sob she knocked it violently to the floor, then turned and ran out of the room.

.Uncle Charlie was still in the kitchen and could only stare at her as she caught his arm and dragged him towards the door. 'She says she's going to marry him! You've got to go and find out for me. He'll tell you—he'll have to tell you. Oh, God, it can't be true, it can't! Please, Uncle Charlie, go and ask him. Make him tell you the truth!'

'Pandora, what is it? *Tell me!*'

Somehow she managed to speak coherently long enough to tell him of her interview with Cynthia Marsden. He listened with a growing frown.

'You'll go and ask him, won't you?' she demanded. 'You don't have to say we're related. You can say it's your right to know if he's dismissed one of the staff. Oh, please, please go and ask him for me!'

'All right. Wait here.' He left with a grim look on his face while Pandora waited in an agony of torment. Within a quarter of an hour he was back.

Heavily, his face averted, he said, 'It's quite true. He's going to make the announcement shortly. And you're to leave tomorrow. He doesn't want to see you again.'

The powerful headlight cut through the swathes of mist that hung over the narrow road between the high stone walls. The night was cold, and the wind made her shiver even though Pandora was wearing her leather jacket and trousers. But perhaps it wasn't the wind, perhaps it was just the shock of having her love thrown back in her face in such a ruthless way. She had insisted on leaving immediately and her uncle had made no move to stop her, even helping her to carry her things to her motorbike and pressing some money on her for the journey, unable to hide the pity and worry in his eyes. Pandora smiled mirthlessly; did they all think that money could buy her off? But that wasn't fair; her uncle had only wanted to make sure that she would be all right until she found somewhere else to stay.

She had no real idea where she was going, had just got on the bike and turned it towards London, which had been an idiotic thing to do because she had been driving for nearly half an hour now and was low on petrol, and there weren't many petrol stations open in the early hours of the morning. All the garages that she passed were closed and part of her mind was beginning to get worried, but mostly she didn't much care; what was one more problem on top of the blows she had already received that night? But when she turned on to the main London road she had only travelled a mile or so when she saw the lights of an all-night garage and pulled into the forecourt. Beside it was a transport café with several large container lorries parked outside, and she decided to go in to get a hot drink to stop herself shivering. And it would be somewhere to sit to pass some of the night away, the endless hours until daylight came and she could start looking for a job and somewhere to live.

Loud punk rock music from the jukebox hit her ears as she pushed open the door. The room was brightly lit and clean enough, with tubular steel tables and chairs, and as this was the only place open for a considerable distance, it was fairly crowded with lorry drivers. There was also a group of leather-clad motorcyclists sitting together at a long table, about eight of them, most of them with long greasy hair and earrings. Pandora hesitated when she saw them, but a quick glance showed her that there were one or two other women in the café, so she stepped inside and went to the counter for a coffee.

She carried her drink to a table as far away from the Hell's Angels as possible, over near the jukebox, and kept her helmet on, hoping they wouldn't notice she was a girl, but they seemed entirely concerned in something they were discussing and hardly gave her a glance. Pandora put her hands round the mug of coffee, trying to warm herself, but after that first, appalling shock and her instinctive reaction to get as far from Abbot's Arbory as possible, a kind of numbness had closed over her and she didn't feel any pain. She was just cold, so cold.

After about twenty minutes or so the music stopped and a couple of the Hell's Angels came over to select some more records. Pandora sat with her back to them, lost in her own unhappiness, oblivious to their conversation, but then the words 'a mile and a half after Arbory Magna' penetrated into her brain and she pricked up her ears.

'I still don't see why we can't go now,' one of the youths was saying. 'If they're having a party or ball, or whatever they call it, they won't notice us going down to the stables.'

'Jess says we've got to wait a bit longer, until they're all either drunk or asleep. Then there won't be anybody to stop us letting them out.' He chuckled coarsely. 'Then we'll chase his bloody horses till they all break their legs, and anybody who gets in the way, too! And serve that toffee-nosed git right for setting the law on to us last time!'

Pandora stared down at her now tepid mug of coffee in dismay. Obviously this was the same gang who had taken their bikes into Abbot's Arbory before and had been arrested for doing so. Pandora didn't know what sort of punishment they had been given, but it was evi-

dent that they intended to get their own back by striking at James through his horses. She thought of
Greymist so near to giving birth to her first foal and her
blood ran cold. She couldn't possibly let it happen. But
what was the best way to prevent it? Her first thought
was to phone the police, but was soon dismissed; she
had only hearsay evidence, no actual crime had been
committed, and they could probably do no more than
warn the gang off, which wouldn't prevent them returning as soon as the police had turned their backs. No,
the best thing she could do was to phone the stables at
Abbot's Arbory and warn them.

There was a public callbox in the entrance to the café,
but the telephone directories were missing and she
couldn't remember the number for Mr Langley's house.
She would have to phone Directory Enquiries to give
her the number, but as she waited for the operator to
answer the gang of youths got up and filed past her on
their way out, and she hastily put the receiver down in a
panic. They must have decided not to wait any longer.
Pandora realised that they would probably cover the
ground to Abbot's Arbory much faster than she had,
would probably take only twenty minutes at the most
to get there. Frantically now she dialled the number for
the house rather than wait for the operator again and
then phone Mr Langley and wait for him to wake up
and answer. She glanced at her watch. Three o'clock.
The ball was due to end at two, but there must surely be
someone up and around still.

Impatiently she waited as she heard the phone ring
over and over again. Come on, somebody answer, she
pleaded silently. Please, please answer! But after another few precious minutes she threw the receiver down
in an agony of exasperation. *Now* what was she going

to do? Then she remembered Jon Thursby and dialled
his number with shaking hands, giving a gasp of relief
when he answered almost at once.

'Jon, it's Pandora. Look, something's happened and
there isn't much time. You must go back to Abbot's
Arbory right away and warn them that a gang of Hell's
Angels are on their way. They intend to let out the
horses and panic them. No, I'm not at the house. It
doesn't *matter* where I am or how I know. *Please*, Jon,
just get over there as fast as you can. They're already on
their way!' Then thankfully she slammed down the receiver as he agreed to go at once.

Pandora ran out to her bike and started it up, intending to follow the gang as fast as she could, but then
remembered that she still needed petrol. Oh, hell! *Why*
couldn't she have got it first? The garage attendant was
inclined to be talkative and get offended when she impatiently snapped at him to hurry up, and deliberately
went slower than ever. Tossing the money at him the
moment he had filled her tank, Pandora tore away
while the man shouted after her that she'd forgotten her
change.

The mist was thicker now, but Pandora drove through
it as fast as she dared, covering the road she had
travelled such a short time ago but with very different
emotions.

When she reached the house and let herself in
through the tradesmen's gate all seemed quiet and
peaceful and she almost began to breathe a sigh of relief
as she coasted silently down the driveway, but then from
the stables came a loud volley of sound, almost like
continuous gunfire, then the high whinneys of frightened horses. Sick with fear, Pandora gunned the bike
into life and tore furiously down the rest of the drive.

As she passed the corner of the house there were more
bangs, and flashes of coloured lights lit the sky inside
the stableyard. With mounting fury she realised that the
gang were using fireworks to further frighten the
animals.

A couple of young colts suddenly galloped out of the
entrance, almost cannoning into her, their nostrils
flailed, their eyes rolling in terror, as they tried to
escape from the fire-crackers tied to their tails. Loud
whoops of laughter followed them and Pandora hastily
drove her bike behind a bush as two youths ran out
after the horses. They didn't see her and went back
again. For a moment Pandora thought of trying to go after
the colts, but Greymist was still inside and she was in
an agony of fear for her. Leaving the bike where it was,
she slid as unobtrusively as possible into the yard,
hoping that if the gang did see her they would mistake
her for one of themselves. They were still at the near
end of the stables, opening the upper doors and sometimes throwing fireworks into the stalls, although one
youth had tied a colt to his bike and was roaring round
and round the yard in decreasing circles with the terrified animal running behind, trying to keep its footing.
As she watched the colt fell and was dragged along for
several yards, screaming and kicking, then it hit one of
its legs against the wall and the screaming stopped as
the poor creature lay still.

Pandora had started to run forward into the open,
her heart filled with a rage so violent that she would
have got hold of the youth and attacked him. Never in
her life had she wanted to hurt anyone, but she could
have killed—*wanted* to kill him. But from behind the
red mists of fury the fear for Greymist held her back,
and she turned and ran back into the shadows and

down to the other end of the stables where the mare was stalled.

The already frightened horse plunged away from her as she opened the doors, but Pandora put up her visor to quieten the animal and held out her hand. The mare came immediately and Pandora led her out, holding her mane. There was no way out of the stableyard other than by the entrance that was blocked by the gang. They had another horse out now, James' black stallion, and were trying to tie a firework to its tail, but the horse reared and bucked, sending one youth flying with a kick from its hindlegs, then it broke free and headed for the entrance.

Good for you, Pandora thought exultantly, and took advantage of them chasing it to vault up on to Greymist's back. 'Come on now, my lovely,' she whispered as she bent low over the mare's neck. 'Don't be afraid. Just one short gallop and you'll be safe.'

Then she pressed her heels gently into the mare's flanks and the quivering animal shot forward as Pandora clung to her mane.

The youths began to shout at her, but they were howls of encouragement as they thought that she was one of the gang and then they jumped hastily out of the way as she rode straight at them, uncaring whether she hit them or not. Another firework went off and Greymist swerved wildly, but Pandora managed to hold on and to keep the mare's head towards the entrance arch. And then they were through and running from the hell the youths had made into the blessed darkness. As soon as they were safely out, Pandora slid off her back and ran alongside the horse down towards the lake. There were lights in the house now and she saw the headlights of a car coming fast down the drive, but she

didn't stop until she reached the summerhouse and per-
suaded the mare inside.

'There now, my beauty, you'll be safe here until I can
get someone to look after you. No, I haven't got any
sugar-lumps. I'm sorry.' This last said almost on a sob
as the mare nuzzled her pockets. 'It's not the night for
sugar-lumps.'

Pandora pulled the heavy doors to and ran back as
hard as she could towards the stables, aware of shouts
as people ran from the house. But she was nearer and
had to try and stop the gang before they hurt any more
of the horses. Sobbing for breath, her chest heaving, she
came to the entrance and looked in again. Her heart
froze as she saw that one of the boxes was on fire, but
even that shock was cancelled out as she heard a bellow
of anger and saw some of the gang fighting a man who
was trying to keep them out of the stalls, and recognised Mr Langley, his hair dishevelled, a pair of trousers
thrown on over his pyjamas.

Without stopping to think, Pandora ran back to
where she had hidden her bike and started it up, pulling
down her visor: if the gang had mistaken her for one of
themselves once, they might do so again. Accelerating
into the centre of the yard, she sounded her horn and
then braked sharply. In as gruff a voice as she could
manage, she shouted, 'Rozzers! They've called the law.
Get out, fast!'

It worked like magic; they let Mr Langley, who was
by now on his knees, go, and ran to their bikes, afraid
of being trapped in the yard. Pandora drove out first
and they immediately followed her. She led them round
the back of the house, away from the people who were
rushing to the stables, past the garage block and up the
back way towards the tradesmen's entrance, then she

turned and headed across the park, an idea suddenly coming into her mind. Like a lot of sheep they followed her, close bunched together. Pandora accelerated, knowing exactly what she was going to do. There was a group of trees ahead of her and she suddenly switched off her lights as she neared them and swerved violently to one side. Turning off her engine, she coasted among the tree trunks. The Hell's Angels, not realising what had happened, roared by, the sound of their engines thundering through the night. A minute later there was a crash of metal and screams of terror as the ground disappeared beneath them and they dropped sickeningly down the drop of the ha-ha. They were packed so closely that there was no time for those at the rear to stop and they fell, bikes and men on top of one another. It wasn't a very deep drop and probably hadn't done them much harm, but it would at least delay them and possibly put some of their bikes out of action and make it easier for the police to catch them. And serve them damn well right! Pandora thought viciously, remembering the colt they'd dragged round the yard.

Turning the bike, she headed back fast towards the stables, terrified that the fire might have spread and Mr Langley and the rest of the horses be trapped inside. But as she neared it there was no glow of flames in the sky, and she prayed that someone had got there and put the fire out. From behind the stables a car appeared, roaring towards her, its headlights blazing. Realising that her lights were still off, Pandora hastily turned them on, but the car kept on coming, its headlights dazzling her. She put up a hand to shield her eyes and pulled as far over to the left as she could, but the car seemed to deliberately turn in the same direction and the next second Pandora's own scream of terror rent the night as she swerved again, hit something, and went hurtling over the handlebars.

She seemed to be flying through the air for a long time, but then she landed on her side on something fairly soft and rolled over and over until she banged her head and came to a stop with a cry of pain. She hurt, everything hurt, and there were mists of pain in front of her eyes. Sluggishly she tried to get up, but fell back again, biting her lip to stop the cry of agony that came to her lips.

Then she heard footsteps and the sound of someone scrambling towards her. A voice, furious with rage, said, 'You young lout! Where are the others? Where are they?' And she opened her eyes to see James towering over her, his face murderous.

He grabbed hold of her shoulders and hauled her to her feet, regardless of her gasp of pain.

'You'll tell me, do you hear?' he thundered. 'Where and who they are. Even if I have to break every bone in your body to find out!'

He was shaking her so hard that she couldn't have answered even if she'd been able to. His hand went to her neck and he almost tore the helmet off her head, throwing it violently to one side.

She heard him give a choking gasp and say her name, but then her legs gave way and she fell against him, trying to fight off black waves of giddiness.

'Pandora!' he gasped again. 'Oh, dear God, what have I done?'

He picked her up and seemed to be carrying her up some sort of bank, and then she felt herself being set down and he let go of her.

'James!' She opened her eyes in a panic, reaching out for him. 'Don't leave me. Please don't leave me.'

'It's all right, darling, I'm here.'

He was at her other side and she realised that he had put her in his car and gone round to the driver's seat. Fiercely she battled against another wave of faintness, clinging tightly to his hand. 'Greymist,' she gasped out. 'We have to get her.'

'We will, my darling, but first I have to get you to a doctor.'

'No, I'm all right. I just banged my head, that's all. Please, James!' She pulled anxiously at his lapel. 'We must go to Greymist. And those men—you must call the police and . . .'

James' hand came up to cover hers. 'They've already been sent for.' He looked at her anxiously, his arm going round her. 'Pandora, are you really all right? If only I'd known it was you—God, I'll never forgive myself for hurting you!'

Somehow she managed to smile at him, although her head felt as if Big Ben was being rung inside it. 'It's all right, I understand. I know you thought I was one of them. I just have a headache.'

'You're sure?'

'Yes. James, Greymist may be having her foal. She was so frightened. We must hurry. And Mr Langley, I know he was hurt.'

'No, he's all right,' he assured her as he started the car and began to turn it. 'He said one of the infernal louts came and shouted that the police were coming and they ran away before they'd done more than knocked him about a bit, thank goodness.' He frowned. 'Although the police haven't got here yet, so how . . .' He broke off and shot her a quick glance. 'Good God, Pandora, was that you?'

'Yes.' She was sitting in the seat, her nails digging

into the upholstery, biting her lip to stop herself from moaning as the car jolted over a dip in the driveway. Nausea rose in her throat, but there was no time to stop the car and be sick, she had to get to Greymist, so somehow she fought it down.

It was only a short distance to the stables, but it seemed to take forever before they pulled up near the entrance. Thankfully Pandora pushed open the door and got out, taking great gulps of the night air.

'Wait here,' James ordered. He turned to go into the stables, but just then Jon Thursby came out with a grim, bitter look on his face.

'I'm sorry, there was no hope of saving the colt. His leg was broken. I've had to put him down.'

'And the other horses?' James asked, his face white.

'There are two still in their stalls that weren't harmed at all. I think Mr Langley managed to stop the gang getting at them, and we've managed to catch three more, but the rest are scattered and probably frightened out of their wits. My God, if I could get my hands on those thugs I'd . . .'

'What about Greymist?' James demanded sharply, cutting through Jon's anger.

He shook his head. 'There's no sign of her.'

'Then we'd better start searching the . . .'

'I know where she is. I took her to the summerhouse,' Pandora cut in impatiently.

James turned to her incredulously. 'You managed to get her out?' His eyes grew warm, and he reached out to touch her face. 'Oh, Pandora!' Then, rather unsteadily, 'Let's go and find her, shall we?'

The brilliant red rays of a summer dawn were lighting the sky when at last Pandora walked rather stiffly out of the summerhouse and down the steps towards the lake, pausing at its edge to listen to the bird song that filled the air and to look at the soft, hazy reflection of the house in the still waters. She felt cramped from sitting for so long with Greymist's head in her lap, continuously talking softly to the still trembling and frightened mare and encouraging it as Jon Thursby had acted as midwife. It had taken a long time for the foal to be born; James had been there with them at first, but the police officers had wanted him for something and he had only returned just before the foal, a colt, was born. Unsteadily the poor little thing had stood up on its impossibly thin, spindly legs, and there had been a wonderful moment of happiness and relief when Jon had pronounced both the colt and Greymist perfectly healthy. The sudden release from tension and worry had made Pandora realise just how tired she was. Her head still ached, but it was nowhere near as painful as it had been when she first came off the bike, and her body wasn't too bad, just bruised and sore in places. But when Greymist had been got on to her feet and had turned her attention to her foal, Pandora had felt suddenly cold and lonely and had quietly slipped outside, leaving the two men talking together.

Behind her she heard the door of the summerhouse open and someone come out. Footsteps came towards her, but she didn't turn round, her body growing tense as James came to stand beside her. He was wearing an overcoat thrown over his dinner jacket and there was a black smudge on his cheek where he had helped to put out the fire in the stables.

He didn't speak at first, and to fill the silence Pandora said as lightly as she could, 'Have you decided on a name for the foal?'

'Not yet. Why don't you choose one for me?'

She looked up at the sky, shot through with the bright crimson rays of the morning, a morning so beautiful that it took your breath away and made you feel incredibly humble and grateful for being alive. Slowly she said, 'Why don't you call him Dawnlight?'

'Dawnlight out of Greymist. Yes, I like it.' She felt him turn to face her. 'Why don't we go up to the house and have a glass of champagne to celebrate his safe arrival?'

She turned away and began to walk towards the stables. 'Thanks, but I have to see how badly my bike's damaged.'

James caught her arm, stopping her. 'Why—so that you can run away from me again?' he demanded, his voice suddenly harsh.

Pandora didn't answer, her face averted.

'Look at me,' James ordered, impatiently pulling her round to face him. 'Why did you run away?'

Slowly Pandora lifted her head. He was staring down at her searchingly, his eyes intent, his brows drawn together in a frown, partly of anger, but there was anxiety behind it too. She gazed at him in growing enlightenment. Wonderingly she said, 'You're—you're *not* going to marry Cynthia Marsden, are you?'

He looked at her in amazement. 'Marry Cynthia? Of course I'm not. Who on earth put that idea in your head?'

Rather slowly Pandora replied, 'She did—and someone else.'

'*No*, I am *not* going to marry her,' James said forcefully. 'I'm not in love with her and never have been. There's only one woman I've ever wanted to be my wife.'

Putting aside that last statement, Pandora said, 'But

she is your mistress, isn't she?'

A rather bleak look came into his face. 'She was, you mean. It was a relationship we drifted into; she made it plain that she was available and I accepted. But I made it clear right from the start that I had no intention of marrying her, it was purely an affair of mutual convenience.'

'Purely?' Pandora demanded on a derisive note.

'All right, impurely, if you like.' James took hold of her shoulders. 'No, don't turn away from me,' he ordered angrily. 'I'm thirty-five years old, Pandora. Did you really expect that I'd have lived like a monk while I waited for the right girl to come along?' Then, at the look on her face, he let her go and said abruptly, 'The affair between Cynthia and me lasted only a short while and ended over a year ago.'

Pandora's head came up quickly at that. 'A year ago? And yet her clothes are still kept in one of the bedrooms here.'

An exasperated look came into his grey eyes. 'Cynthia's parents often go away and she's afraid to stay in the house alone since they had a burglary recently, so they asked me if I'd let her stay here on the nights they were away. Her people are old family friends and in the circumstances I was unable to refuse, but I always made sure that the housekeeper was around to act as chaperone. And last month—at the dinner party when you cooked for us—I made sure that my aunt came along so that Cynthia wouldn't get any ideas about staying the night. That—and because I wanted my aunt to meet you.'

Pandora's eyes widened. 'Why should you want your aunt to meet me?'

He smiled. 'What man doesn't want to show off the girl he loves to his relatives?'

She flushed and would have lowered her head, but

James put his hand under her chin, forcing her to look at him. 'Darling, how could you have believed Cynthia when I'd already told you that I loved you?'

'It wasn't only Cynthia. And besides . . .' she hesitated and then added with difficulty, 'that evening in your bedroom—do you remember?'

His eyes grew warm. 'How could I ever forget?'

'Well, the phone rang.'

'Mm.' His arm went round her waist and he drew her closer. 'Just in time to stop me from losing control of myself completely.' Pandora put her hands against his chest, holding herself away from him, and his eyes grew serious again. 'Go on.'

The pain raw in her voice, Pandora said, 'You answered the phone and said you had to go out. Later that night I met your chauffeur. He—he said he'd taken you to Cynthia's house and that—and that you were staying the night.'

James swore, and she could feel his hands tighten on her waist as he said earnestly, 'It wasn't Cynthia who phoned; it was her father. We're both on the board of the local hospital and he asked me to go round there and discuss something before the next meeting. I sent the car back because I wanted to walk home—I wanted some time to be alone, to think about you and about the future. And,' he hesitated a moment and added slowly, 'and most of all to wonder if I'd made you aware enough of your own feelings to follow your heart and not your head, and accept my proposal when I asked you to marry me the next day.' His voice changed. 'Only you didn't come the next morning as you'd promised. Instead you went to Oxford and didn't come back until the early hours, while I went through hell wondering if I'd frightened you away.' Gently his hand came up to cup her chin. 'And all the time it was because you thought I'd been with Cynthia.' His eyes warmed. 'Well, at least it proves that I was right. You did love me then.'

Pandora smiled rather tremblingly. 'I only realised it that evening. And then—afterwards—I thought that you were just playing with me, amusing yourself by trying to seduce me. I couldn't understand why else you kept—kept kissing me and . . .' Her voice trailed away and she blushed.

James smiled. 'I think the phrase you want is "making love to you".' Adding rather ruefully, 'Darling, what other choice did I have? After your outburst that day in Oxford you'd made it perfectly plain just what you thought of my position and way of life. If I'd tried to get closer to you by normal means—by asking you out and introducing you to my circle of friends—you'd have refused point blank. Also the fact that you'd put on that act to start with showed that you were on the defensive against me, and more than ready to rebuff me if I made the slightest approach towards you. So I reasoned that the only chance I had was to get under your guard and try to awaken your emotions enough to unsettle you thoroughly so that you didn't know your own mind any more.' He bent and gently began to explore her eyelids with his lips. 'I had an idea, you see, that you'd never been awakened before. You were like a rosebud waiting for the kiss of the sun before you opened your petals.'

He lifted his head to look at her and Pandora slowly opened her eyes. His voice changed, grew grim again. 'It came as quite a shock when you told me that you thought nothing of sleeping around.'

Pandora blushed. 'I don't—I mean it wasn't—I

haven't . . .' She came to a floundering stop, her cheeks crimson, and looked up quickly as James laughed.

'Do you think I didn't realise that when I'd had time to cool off and think about it? Oh, Pandora,' his arms went round her and he drew her close, moulding her body against his, 'do you know how long I've waited for a girl like you to come along? A girl with innocence in her eyes and who can find joy in simple things? Who can dance barefoot in the grass and fill her arms with flowers? Oh, darling!' he bent to kiss her gently. 'I've read of men who fell in love at first sight, but I never thought it would happen to me, and then I looked out of my window one morning and saw you.' He chuckled softly. 'At first I couldn't believe that you were real. I thought I'd fallen in love with a ghost.'

Pandora put up a tentative finger to trace the outline of his lips. 'But I'm very real.'

His arms tightened convulsively. 'I know *that*. Oh, God, Pandora, if you only knew how much I wanted you!' His mouth found hers, kissing her with a fierce hunger that was scarcely controlled and would not long be denied, and for the first time Pandora was able to respond with complete abandon, letting her emotions guide her and moving sensuously against him, longing to be a part of him.

Uncle Charlie, she thought bemusedly, when at last she could think more coherently. So that story of his about James not wanting to see her again had been as fictional as Cynthia Marsden's; her uncle had been so convinced that James had no serious intentions towards her, that he would only hurt her, that like Cynthia, he was prepared to stop at nothing to prevent his niece getting badly hurt. In any other circumstances Pandora would have been furiously angry—but now she could only try to see Uncle Charlie's point of view, and thank heaven he had done no lasting damage by his well-intentioned lie!

How long they stood in each other's arms, Pandora didn't know, but when she next became aware of her surroundings the sun had turned to gold and was quite high in the sky. The mist had disappeared, and summer lay across the house and park like a lover's embrace, warm and caressing. Pandora looked at it and caught her breath in wonder, still unable to believe that her future lay here. She turned a radiant, mischievous face up to the man she loved.

'You do realise that I'm only marrying you because I've fallen in love with Abbot's Arbory?'

'Of course,' James agreed gravely, as he stooped to pick her up in his arms and carry her back to the house, 'that's understood. And you know that I'm only marrying you because I can't stand Richardson's everlasting omelettes any longer, don't you?'

Pandora put her arms round his neck and gurgled with laughter. 'Oh, that reminds me,' she said happily, 'there's something I have to tell you. It's about my Uncle Charlie . . .'

The Mills & Boon Rose is the Rose of Romance

Every month there are ten new titles to choose from — ten new stories about people falling in love, people you want to read about, people in exciting, far-away places. Choose Mills & Boon. It's your way of relaxing:

July's titles are:

SUMMER FIRE *by Sally Wentworth*
Why had Pandora ensured that the haughty but charming Sir James Arbory would never look at her twice?

CASTLES OF SAND *by Anne Mather*
Little Hussein was Ashley's son, but she must never let him know who she was. How could she put up with the hostility of Hussein's formidable uncle Alain . . .

SPITFIRE *by Lindsay Armstrong*
Rod Simpson had bought Bobbie's home and let her stay there. But what happened when his sister got married and went away?

STRANGERS INTO LOVERS *by Lilian Peake*
There was nothing between Gillian Taylor and Randall West any more, except two people, one who loved Gillian and another who loved Randall. And of course, Gary . . .

ABDUCTION *by Charlotte Lamb*
The worst thing that had happened to Marisa was for her baby to be snatched. It also brought her estranged husband Gabriel back on the scene . . .

ONE OF THE BOYS *by Janet Dailey*
Petra Wallis fell in love with her boss, the dominating Dane Kingston. But he had no more use for her as a woman than as a technician . . .

THE FLAME OF DESIRE *by Carole Mortimer*
Sophie's marriage to Luke Vittorio was a mockery. She had the best of reasons for knowing he was still having an affair with her stepmother . . .

THE SAVAGE TOUCH *by Helen Bianchin*
Lee was very much attracted to Marc Leone. But nothing was going to deflect her from her real goal in life: to marry a millionaire! ·

MIXED FEELINGS *by Kerry Allyne*
Kylie's boss, Grant Brandon, was old enough to be her father. So there was no need for his disagreeable nephew, Race Brandon, to be so scathing about her!

A TASTE OF PARADISE *by Margaret Mayo*
Her fiancé had not told Cathy about the unyielding Grant Howard, who lived on the island she had received as a wedding present . . .

If you have difficulty in obtaining any of these books from your local paperback retailer, write to:

Mills & Boon Reader Service
P.O. Box 236, Thornton Road, Croydon, Surrey, CR9 3RU.

The Mills & Boon Rose is the Rose of Romance

COLLISION *by Margaret Pargeter*
After the heartless way Max Heger had treated her, Selena wanted to be revenged on him. But things didn't work out as she had planned.

DARK REMEMBRANCE *by Daphne Clair*
Could Raina marry Logan Thorne a year after her husband Perry's death, when she knew that Perry would always come first with her?

AN APPLE FROM EVE *by Betty Neels*
Doctor Tane van Diederijk and his fiancée were always cropping up in Euphemia's life. If only she could see the back of both of them?

COPPER LAKE *by Kay Thorpe*
Everything was conspiring to get Toni engaged to Sean. But she was in love with his brother Rafe — who had the worst possible opinion of her!

INVISIBLE WIFE *by Jane Arbor*
Vicente Massimo blamed Tania for his brother's death. So how was it that Tania soon found herself blackmailed into marrying him?

BACHELOR'S WIFE *by Jessica Steele*
Penny's marriage to Nash Devereux had been a ' paper ' one. So why did Nash want a reconciliation just when Penny wanted to marry Trevor?

CASTLE IN SPAIN *by Margaret Rome*
Did Birdie love the lordly Vulcan, Conde de la Conquista de Retz — who wanted to marry her — or did she fear him?

KING OF CULLA *by Sally Wentworth*
After the death of her sister, Marnie wanted to be left alone. But the forceful Ewan McNeill didn't seem to get the message!

ALWAYS THE BOSS *by Victoria Gordon*
The formidable Conan Garth was wrong in every opinion he held of Dinah — but could she ever make him see it?

CONFIRMED BACHELOR *by Roberta Leigh*
Bradley Dexter was everything Robyn disliked. But now that she could give him a well-deserved lesson, fate was playing tricks on her!

Masquerade
Historical Romances

Intrigue excitement romance

THE EAGLE'S FATE
by Dinah Dean

When Napoleon invaded Russia, Nadya had to walk from Moscow with her possessions on her back. She expected pity from Captain Andrei Valyev, but he seemed to hate her — why, then, had he rescued her from a fate worse than death?

MAN WITH A FALCON
by Caroline Martin

Richenda rather welcomed the excitement when the Civil War came to the very gates of her home, Black Castle. But that was before she had encountered the Royalist leader, Sebastian, Lord Devenish!

Look out for these titles in your local paperback shop from 10th July 1981

From this month three great Doctor Nurse Romances

From July on, Mills & Boon publish an extra title in this very popular collection. Each month, there are three for you to look out for and enjoy. These are the titles for July

ALL FOR CAROLINE
by Sarah Franklin

Megan Lacey takes up the job of speech therapist simply as a way of avenging her cousin's broken heart. But she makes a complete mess of things — and loses her own heart into the bargain.

THE SISTER AND THE SURGEON
by Lynne Collins

Sister Ruth Challis is amazed to find her cold heart melting towards untrustworthy consultant, Oliver Manning, but complications increase when her old friend Daniel's feelings about her become significant . . .

SOUTH ISLAND NURSE
by Belinda Dell

When both the Senior Medical Registrar, Sandy Legrady, and the new house physician, Ian Dugall, vie for her attention, Staff Nurse Erica Ryall is forced to juggle with their affections . . .